if

you

only

knew

LOOK FOR MORE BOOKS ABOUT
**THE FRIENDSHIP RING:**

please, please, please (C.J.'s story)

not that i care (Morgan's story)

**THE**
**FRIENDSHIP**
**RING**

*Rachel Vail*

if

you

only

knew

**SCHOLASTIC PRESS    NEW YORK**

Published by Scholastic Press, a division of Scholastic Inc., *Publishers since 1920*.
SCHOLASTIC and SCHOLASTIC PRESS and associated logos are trademarks or registered
trademarks of Scholastic Inc.

Library of Congress Cataloging-in-Publication Data

Vail, Rachel.
If you only knew / by Rachel Vail.
p.   cm. — (The friendship ring)
Summary: Seventh-grader Zoe, who comes from a big family where she's never had
anything all to herself, desperately wants CJ for a best friend, but when CJ reveals that
she likes the boy Zoe likes, she must make a choice.
ISBN 0-590-03370-0
[1. Friendship—Fiction. 2. Interpersonal relations—Fiction. 3. Schools—Fiction. 4.
Family life—Fiction.] I. Title. II. Series: Vail, Rachel. Friendship ring.
PZ7.V1916If 1998        97-32548      [Fic]—dc21      CIP      AC

12 11 10 9 8 7 6 5 4 3 2 1        8 9/9 0/0 01 02 03

Printed in the U.S.A.   36
First Edition, July 1998
The text type was set in 12-point Dante Medium.
Book design by David Saylor

to

Lil and Bill Vail,

best friends

forever

if

you

only

knew

## one

When you're the youngest of five girls, nothing's your own. I share a room with my sister Devin, and most of my clothes used to be hers. The first day of school, teachers say, "Oh, another Grandon," instead of just, "Hello, Zoe." I have my sister Bay's hair and my sister Anne Marie's mouth and, unfortunately, my mother's behind. I doubt if I've ever had an original thought.

That was all fine with me until tonight.

I'm friends with everybody in my grade, including the boys. I haven't been asked out yet — maybe I'm too tall or too good friends with them or something. Doesn't bother me, though. Last year nobody tried to kiss me, but just about everybody passed me notes.

I've never had a best friend, either, never really saw the point. I like to hang out with lots of different people. Why limit myself? But here I am, lying in the dark, plotting how to make CJ Hurley choose me as her best friend.

We're having a sleepover at her house, which is partly why I'm still awake — it's cold. They have air-conditioning but no yelling, the opposite of us. When their mother said, "Bedtime," CJ and her little brother ran straight to the bathroom and started brushing. That was a surprise. I got up and rushed in after them; I hate to be left out and besides, what could I do? Stay and bargain for a few more minutes with somebody else's parents?

CJ has her own room and an extra bed that pops out from under hers just for sleepovers. We put on our

T-shirts and boxers, turned out the light, and lay here for I don't know how long. I was thinking, *Well, this is weird. Devin and I always talk in the dark of our room. I can't just go to sleep.*

"Are you asleep?" I whispered to CJ.

"No," she whispered back.

"Just wondering." I have good eyes — the best in my family — so I checked out CJ's built-in shelves across the room. She has a collection of stuffed animals lined up neatly, like they're not to play with anymore.

"Don't feel bad about tonight," she whispered.

"I had a great time," I said, which was true. I love barbecues — the smell of the hot dogs on the grill, your hair still wet from the shower, playing catch in the swim club parking lot until it gets too dark to see. "Didn't you have fun?" I asked her.

"Yeah, but when you went out to the parking lot with the boys . . ."

"We were playing catch."

"You were the only girl," she said. "I thought maybe you . . ."

"You could've come." I felt bad suddenly that I hadn't invited her. But nobody invited me. I just went. If she'd wanted to come, she should've come.

"I thought you felt left out or something. With the girls."

"Girls?" her father called as he passed CJ's door.

"Sorry," CJ said.

He turned off the bathroom light and said, "Good night."

"I didn't feel left out," I whispered. "I just felt like playing catch."

"Shh," she whispered back. Like we were in trouble. Boy, in my house, trouble is a lot louder than that.

The light from her parents' room shut off. Maybe a minute later, CJ lifted her head up again and leaned on her elbow. "How does it feel to have four older sisters?"

I shrugged. "How does it feel not to?"

"I mean, is it like a party all the time? That's probably why you get along with everybody — you've just always had to. Or do you wish you could have more privacy?"

"I don't really like privacy," I said. "It's boring."

"That's so funny." She pushed her blanket down and lifted her leg up to her face. She's a ballerina so she can. "If I don't have time to myself, I go crazy."

"If I kissed my knee like that, my leg would pop off."

"You get used to it," she said.

I shrugged. "Same with sisters, I guess."

She switched legs. "But are they into your things all the time? My brother used my markers yesterday, and I could yank his little fingernails out."

"Ouch," I said. "I never thought about it before, really. My sister Colette gets a little weird about people touching her CDs, but she's the difficult one. I don't mind much. I mean, practically everything of mine was one of theirs first, so what do I care?"

She nodded sympathetically. "You must be dying to have something that's just your own."

"Well, I have . . ." I started but I couldn't finish because I couldn't think of anything. "I have . . ." Nothing. Nothing of my own? "I'm the only one who doesn't go in alphabetical order," I finally came up with.

"What do you mean?" She splayed her legs into a split and propped up her head in her palms, in between. She wasn't wearing a bun for the first time I'd ever seen, and her pale bony face looked lost in the frizz of all that brown fluffy hair.

"That doesn't hurt your legs?" I had to ask.

She shook her head. She was just waiting for me to talk. That felt pretty nice — at my house you have to talk fast if you have something to say or somebody else will fill in with a different story.

"They had a kid a year for four years," I explained. "A-B-C-D: Anne Marie, Bay, Colette, and Devin. Then the next year a dog, Elvis. And then me. But my mom was like, no way is this one Fiona, don't even think I'm going through this twenty more times; this kid is named Zoe. As in, The End."

"Well, that is sort of alphabetical," CJ said.

"No. You get it? Z."

"Just with a lot of letters skipped."

"Oh." I could see what she meant. "Thanks for pointing that out."

"I'm sorry."

"Great," I said, "the one thing I thought was my own."

She shook her head slowly and whispered, "That must feel awful."

Nobody ever took me so seriously in my life. Not even myself. I could hear my sisters saying, *Oh, please, get over yourself. So what? Alphabetical order? Please.* But interrupting their voices in my head was CJ, saying, *That must feel awful.* And it did. "It does," I whispered back. "It feels awful."

"I know it," she said. She talks really slow.

Her sympathy felt so good, I wanted to give her gifts. "Thanks," I said. I had to laugh at myself. "I don't know what's wrong with me. I'm not usually such a sap."

"No, seriously," she said. "It's so hard. I know just how you feel. I mean, the same with my mom about ballet — I tried to tell her I'm not sure if I want to dance this year, and she didn't even hear me. She's just writing out the check anyway, saying, 'You're so gifted, you're so talented,' blah, blah, blah."

I nodded. I thought about saying *that must feel awful* back to her but I didn't want to copy. Also, it didn't sound awful. I can't imagine my mother saying anything that nice to me. The closest she comes is, *At least you're no trouble.* So I told CJ, "Maybe she's just really proud of you."

"Maybe." She lay down on her side and whispered, "My real name is Cornelia Jane, same as my mom."

"I know," I said. "Mrs. Platt?" We were in homeroom together last year and the teacher, Mrs. Platt, always called CJ, Cornelia Jane, Our Prima Ballerina — even when she was just taking attendance.

"Oh, yeah," CJ said, scrunching her pointy little nose. "It's a family name. My great-grandmother was called Lia, then Grandma is Nelly, and my mom is Corey, so I guess they ran out of nicknames that were actual names, for me."

"I like CJ."

"Really?"

"Usually only boys get initial nicknames."

"Exactly," she said, flopping down flat on the bed.

Wrong thing to say. Oops. I tried something else. "That's great, to have the same name as your mother. The only thing I have in common with my mother is a weight problem."

She didn't take her arm off her face. "It's not that great, actually," she said in that slow way of hers.

"Oh," I said.

"When I was little, I could only touch her toe shoes if I first washed my hands with soap. That's why I started ballet — I wanted toe shoes I could touch anytime. And to be just like her."

"No wonder she's psyched you're so good," I said. CJ is a really talented dancer. Last year we had a class trip to see her in *The Nutcracker*. When she came out to the lobby afterward, we were pulling on our wool sweaters and down coats. She looked like a different species from us. You could understand why people who perform are called stars. She sparkled, practically. On the bus ride home, some people said it was just the special makeup with glitter in it, but I don't think so.

CJ pushed her blanket away again and stretched her neck so her head reached her knees. "Four days a week she drives me all the way to Lenox for lessons and sits there watching me for three hours."

"That's great," I said.

"I guess so," she told her knees.

"What do you mean?" I asked. "All that time, just for you? Once, when I was like, four, my mom took me to *Sesame Street Live,* just the two of us, and bought me an Elmo flashlight. Please, it's still my favorite thing."

"I don't know, never mind," CJ said, sitting up and hugging her knees.

"What?"

"Sometimes I just want . . ."

"What?" I asked. "You can tell me." I sat up, too. I love secrets.

"You'll think it's stupid."

"I won't. I promise."

"OK. Sometimes I wish I could just hang around the pizza place after school instead of dancing."

I thought that was pretty stupid so I stayed still.

CJ frowned. "Stupid, right?"

"No," I had to lie. "But you know what? Their pizza isn't even crisp."

"I don't care."

"And nobody gives you a standing ovation for finishing a slice."

She shook her head. "I'm missing it," she whispered. "All the regular stuff. I don't think I'll ever be good enough to make principal dancer, so I'm just wasting —"

"Maybe you will," I interrupted. "You're really good."

"You don't know. I'm good but my turn-out isn't enough and meanwhile I'm missing being a normal kid."

We lay there in the dark for a minute. She was right, how could I know if she's good? She looked great to me last year, but I don't even know what turn-out is.

"That must feel awful," I whispered.

"It does," she said. She started to cry.

Oops, wrong thing again. It had felt so good when she said it to me. I looked around for Kleenex, but she didn't have a box. "You want me to get you some toilet paper?"

"For what?"

"To wipe your nose? Eyes?" I asked. "I don't know what to do."

"Some toilet paper?" She wiped her face on her T-shirt. "It's OK."

"So what are you going to do?" I asked. "About dance."

"There's nothing I can do, because it's not up to me, it's obviously my mother's decision. Anyway, the point is, I know just how you feel, about nothing of your own."

I nodded. I never know what to say when people get serious.

"Morgan says I should just quit. But she doesn't care about stuff like disappointing your mother. I mean, my mother's always telling me I'm her best friend."

I stopped myself from saying that's so nice. Instead I said, "Oh, that makes it complicated."

I wasn't even sure what I meant, but I was glad I said it because CJ nodded fast, looking right at me. She has really intense green eyes. "Exactly," she said. "See? Morgan doesn't get that — she doesn't care what her

mother thinks. But on the other hand, Morgan is right —
it is my decision, really. Whether to dance and even who
my best friend is. My mom can't just decide we're best
friends. Don't I have some say?"

"Absolutely," I said.

She nodded more and smiled a little. "I mean *best*
friends — it's too important. It's a commitment, right?
Best friends have to choose each other."

"Yeah," I said. "I agree."

"I'm glad somebody does," whispered CJ.

"Who's your best friend, then? Morgan?" CJ and Morgan Miller hung around a lot last year. I guess I thought
of them as best friends. I was regular friends with both of
them, although since *The Nutcracker,* I've been a little shy
around CJ. It's hard to imagine all my friends needing
permission slips to come see me do anything.

"Well," CJ said slowly. "I was best friends with Gideon Weld when we were little, but then, you know, we figured out he was a boy and I was a girl, so that ended that."

"Right," I said, like obviously you couldn't be best friends with a boy. I'm just friends with anybody. Nothing of my own. Why didn't that ever bother me before?

"And since fourth grade, it's been Morgan, although, sometimes, lately, I feel like she doesn't understand me," CJ whispered. "But yeah, I guess it's Morgan. Who's yours?"

"I don't know." I faced away from her, toward the door, and folded my pillow over. "I don't have one."

After a while, CJ whispered, "We should go to sleep, huh?"

I said, "Yeah," but I can't sleep.

## two

"**S**eventh grade is the most horrible year," Devin confided, plunging her hand into the soapsuds to open the drain. It was our turn to do the dishes.

"Really? How come?" I can always trust Devin out of all my sisters to tell me the truth and not baby me.

"And you're gonna be all alone," she continued. "At least Colette was around for me. I mean, it was Colette, but still, once I had to go to the girls' room and cry? She cut English and stayed with me the whole period."

"Well, I don't cry in school." I dried my hands on the bottom half of her towel.

She smiled. "Just wait till the hormones kick in." Devin has the best smile in the family. I've tried imitating it in the mirror but mine is big and goofy-looking.

"What does it feel like, when they kick in?" I asked, following her up the steps to our room.

"You'll know. You won't recognize yourself."

"Yikes. Really?"

"Where were you today?"

"CJ Hurley's." Then I decided to try something out, see how it sounded. "She's my best friend."

"Yeah?" Devin sat down on her bed and crossed her legs. "Since when?"

Um. "Recently," I answered. I pulled on my baggiest shorts, Devin's old green ones. "What did you do?"

"Did Colette tell you what she did?" Devin asked.

"No."

Devin smiled. "Never mind, then."

"Come on!" I hate not knowing stuff.

"I promised not to say," Devin said, shrugging. "But after she came home, Anne Marie took us all over to Sundries for school supplies."

"You didn't go with your friends?" I asked.

Devin shook her head. "Mommy gave us money."

"She gave me some to go with my friends tomorrow," I said. "Anne Marie didn't say anything to me. Did you guys get pizza after?"

"Yeah." Devin smiled her little half-smile. "You could've come."

"Yeah, well," I said, digging in my closet for my tennis racquet. The whole family used to go for school supplies together, and then Mom would take us for pizza, after. It was a total free-for-all, everybody with lists and packs of pens. One time they left me there by mistake, and I didn't even notice, I was so busy examining erasers. I loved the whole excitement of it, like these blank notebooks were a fresh start, and if my sisters helped me choose, I would be able to look down at the fading blue of my spiral later in the year like during a tough math quiz and remember Anne Marie thought this was a good notebook. It gave me courage or at least company. But then last year, my sisters got too old and wanted to go with their friends. I didn't want to seem like a baby, so I made a whole thing of going with my friends this year, but I definitely would've gone with my sisters today, if I knew they were all going together. CJ and I were just hanging around in her backyard. At the time it was fun to me, but I didn't realize I was missing everything at home.

"I'm sorry," Devin said. "Don't be sad."

"I don't care." I leaned farther into the closet so Devin wouldn't see how disappointed I was.

"You're not wearing that, are you?"

She was pointing at my sweatshirt, I saw when I looked up. I explained, "It's Big Blue."

"You get very attached to things," Devin observed.

I pulled out my racquet and a can of balls. "Only some things. Feel how soft Big Blue is."

She held up her hand. "Thanks anyway. I guess when I was your age I got attached to physical things, too. It's like a pre-boy stage."

"You're so mature." She's a whole twenty-two months older.

"Amazing, isn't it?" She shrugged. "You're not going over to bother Tommy again, are you?"

"He needs work on his serve." Tommy Levit and I have been hitting off his garage all summer. "Why? What are you doing?" I didn't want to miss more.

"You ought to play a little hard to get, don't you think?"

"He's my buddy." I sat down on my bed, wondering, *Does she know that I've been thinking about Tommy more than usual?*

"You know you flirt with him."

"I do not!" I insisted. Everything is the same. I refuse to go boy-crazy like my sisters, just because Tommy has deep dimples. Just because I get distracted by how cute his face is, lately. "It's not flirting, it's joking," I told Devin. "We're friends."

"That's what I mean, you let him be just friends. Where does that get you?"

"I don't want to get anywhere. Except outside, to practice." I retied my shoe to avoid Devin's eyes. Maybe I really do want more privacy. I can't even have feelings to myself without somebody spying on them.

"Then the hormones definitely haven't kicked in." Devin sat down next to me and started to French-braid her hair.

"Whatever." On my way out, I asked, "Is that a pimple?"

"Where?"

I could hear her scrambling over to her mirror before I reached the stairs. Serves her right. Sometimes I am not as nice a person as I should be. I looked for Colette to find out what she had done but I guess she was Out, her favorite place to go, wherever that is. Probably her skanky boyfriend's.

To get to Tommy and Jonas's house, you just cut across our backyard, climb the fence, and cross their grass. On my way, I wondered if maybe I do have a best friend, and it's Tommy. There's no commitment, like CJ was saying, but Tommy and I rag on each other all the time, and when I'm with him I'm always in a good mood, although nervous, lately, too. But even the nervous is in a good way.

Mrs. Levit answered the door and yelled to Tommy that I was there. I waited in the front hall. She smiled at me but didn't say anything. I smiled back and then looked at my racquet head balancing on the toe of my sneaker. Mrs. Levit was holding hands with herself. When I looked up, she was still smiling at me.

"How are you?" I asked, to be polite.

"Not so great," she said. "I have cramps."

"Oh, that's terrible," I said.

"You're telling me."

I looked up the steps for Tommy, but he was slow as always. I hate getting trapped in his foyer like this. "Did you go to the doctor?"

"No." Mrs. Levit sighed. "It's menstrual."

"Oh," I said.

"Do you get cramps, Zoe?"

"No," I said quickly. Every time I see Mrs. Levit she tells me about her period. It gives me the creeps. My mother can't even say period at the end of a sentence. She says *Point;* the other kind she just calls *That Time.*

"You're lucky, then," Mrs. Levit said. "My uterus . . ."

"Tommy?" I yelled.

Tommy jumped down to the landing and said, "Hey."

"Want to hit?" What I was thinking was, *Get me out of here.*

"Yeah. Hold on." He ran back upstairs, then yelled, "Ma? Where are my sneakers?"

"In the mudroom," she answered. "So anyway . . ."

"I can wait outside," I suggested.

"Are you excited for seventh grade?"

"Not so much," I mumbled.

"I don't blame you. What a rough time."

"Thanks," I said. I don't know why I thanked her. Sometimes I just say thank you when it seems like somebody should say something.

By the time Tommy got outside, I was already in a good volley with myself. He sat on the curb and waited.

"Did you get school supplies yet?" I asked him, mid-backswing.

"No."

Forehand. "I'm going tomorrow with some people, if you and Jonas want to come."

"OK."

"I don't go with my sisters anymore." I caught the tennis ball and tossed it to him. He stood up and walked to the crack we use as a baseline. Before he finished his toss, I asked, "Who's your best friend?"

He served.

"Out," I said.

"Yeah?" He ran for the ball and caught it near the bushes. "Jonas, I guess."

"Oh." Jonas is his twin brother, so I said, "Obviously. But I meant, anybody else?"

He lined up his toe again. "Not really," he said, and tossed. His serve went in that time.

We hit for a while, until it got dark, then sat down on his sidewalk curb again and picked at our blisters. "Well," I said when I was done with mine. "See you at the bus stop tomorrow."

"Yup." He stood up and headed toward his house.

"Tommy?"

He spun around. His black-brown eyes moved up my body, from my sneakers to my bust to my face. I quickly sat down on the curb, because my fingers and toes started prickling the way they did right before I fainted last year as stitches were being removed from my chin. Whoa. When did he turn so cute?

"Did you think that was weird, yesterday?" I managed to ask.

"What?" He pushed the sweaty dark hair off his forehead, leaving a smudge of dirt up his face. I mean, he put a worm on my head in kindergarten. I helped him with his soapbox derby car for Cub Scouts. I know about his mother's menstrual problems. He's practically my brother. But now when I think about the time he kissed Morgan Miller in his tree house last year, I imagine it was me. I wouldn't break up with him for kissing.

"What?" he asked again.

"That I played catch with you guys? Instead of staying with the girls?"

"No." He made a face like, *What a stupid question.* That's what I like about him. He's very no-bull. I guess he gets that from his mom.

"Just wondering."

"Because you're not, like, a girl," he said.

"Really? I'm not?" I wasn't sure if that was a compliment or an insult. "Well, won't my dad be psyched."

"No," he said. He twirled his grip in his palms so the racquet spun. I taught him how to do that in July. "Like, you don't care how you look, and stuff."

"Thanks," I said. I pulled my ponytail tighter. I don't think about how I look all the time, it's true, but I do care. Of course I care.

"In a good way," Tommy said. "Like, you're not all whispery. You're more like one of the guys."

"Oh," I said. "Just wondering." I rested one foot on top of the other. When Devin does that, she looks cute. I wanted him to notice me, differently. That I'm not totally one of the guys.

"Besides, you have a better arm than most of us."

"Thanks," I said. I tried to flash him one of Devin's half-smiles, slowly spreading across my face, slyly like she does it. It felt sort of fake, though, and ended up turning into just my own smile, showing too much of my gums, probably.

He smiled back. "But your forehand wobbles."

"In your dreams," I answered.

He ran toward his door, grinning that sarcastic grin of his.

On my way back over the fence, I scraped my leg, and the blood made tracks through the dirt on its way down to my sock. I tried to decide if it looked tough or just gross. Why should I care if my leg is all scabby for the first day of school? I bent down to inspect it and ended up just spacing, sitting in my yard.

I'm one of the guys, he said. Well, I've always felt like it's a lot better to be a tomboy than a priss. I can't go back on that now.

Some things I guess I do keep private.

## three

Seventh grade. My eyes popped open — I didn't want to be last in the shower and freeze. I jumped up and made my bed in one motion. Who cares what Devin says? Just because seventh grade was the worst for her, I decided, doesn't mean it will be worst for me.

I grabbed my towel and ran down the hall. I was halfway naked by the time Anne Marie opened the bathroom door.

"Come on," Anne Marie tried.

"Sorry." I turned on the water and stepped into the shower. Nice and hot. I let myself enjoy it for a second, then made it cooler so Devin, who's always last in, wouldn't be an icicle on the first day of school.

"You know," said Anne Marie, "this is my last first day."

"What?" I knew without looking that she was sitting on the toilet seat, her towel folded in her lap. It's almost always between me and Anne Marie for second shower (Dad gets up in the dark), and whoever loses sits on the toilet and talks.

"The last first day of school I'll be here," she said. I had heard her fine the first time. I'd never considered it before — this was the last first day of school all the Grandon girls would have together, because next year Anne Marie would be away at college.

"Yeah," I said. I kept my eyes closed so no soap would get in while I rinsed.

Usually we talk straight through, but she didn't say anything else, and I didn't, either. I decided to put off thinking about how different next year will be without Anne Marie, who really runs things around here. I can't deal with more than one trauma at a time. Right then I had to get ready for the first day of middle school alone.

I turned off the water and grabbed the towel Anne Marie shoved in for me. While I dried myself and she showered, I asked, "Was seventh grade your worst year?"

"I don't know," she answered. "Um . . . eighth, I think. Yeah, eighth."

"How come?"

"Oh, everything. Pimples. Remember my chin?"

"Yeah."

"Thank you. Plus I was all jagged edges, and life felt so fragile. I was, like, barbed wire, and life was like panty hose I tried to slip through, but it was always catching on me. Maybe I should write a poem."

"Yeah," I said. "You should." She won English student of the month twice last year. She's very deep and poetic. I wasn't sure what she meant; I'm just regular. Besides, I haven't worn panty hose that much.

"Plus Bay made starter on soccer, and I sat on the bench," she added.

"You didn't play?" I was surprised.

"Barely," she said. "And my little sister got MVP. Ugh. Be glad you're not in eighth grade."

"I don't remember you sitting on the bench," I said.

She turned off the water. I pushed her towel in past the shower curtain. "How could you remember?" she asked, taking the towel. "You were a baby."

We walked back down the hall to our rooms. My black jeans were a little tight from the dryer but the scab on my knee was pretty gross-looking, so shorts were out. I like to wear pink on the first day of school because it seems like a friendly color, so I took out Devin's old oversized pink T-shirt, which I'd been saving. I do care how I look.

I combed my hair, sitting on the bed to fight the knots (and stretch out the jeans), and thought about what Anne Marie had said. I was a baby. I wondered how much else I had missed. I hate missing stuff. But then I smelled French toast so I stopped thinking. I jammed my feet into my sneakers and skidded down the steps. Devin was hitting her snooze again.

"Save some for me," Bay yelled from the shower.

"No way!" Anne Marie yelled, right behind me. My dad makes amazing French toast. He's a baker and totally obsessed with bread. Anytime we go on a vacation, it's always to someplace with brick ovens or yeast.

I was on my second piece and Bay had just finished her first when Colette drifted down. She filled a glass with water and sat in her seat next to me. Dad plopped a big piece of French toast onto her plate.

"No, thank you," Colette said.

Dad's smile stiffened a little. "I made it special, on my best barley bread. Good start to your first day."

"I'm on a diet," Colette said, sipping her water. I bent my head down and ate a huge hunk of French toast and thought, *No, no, no.*

"You are not going to school until that French toast is eaten," Dad enunciated. His fists were on the table, with the spatula gripped tight in one of them. I didn't dare look up at his face.

Next to me, Colette leaned back in her chair and crossed her arms over her tight T-shirt. Her words, like Dad's, get superarticulated when they're starting one of their fights. "Fine," she said, chiseling each sound, "then I won't go to school."

"Morning!" Devin ran into the dining room upside down, flipping her head to gather her wet hair into a ponytail. "Mmm, yum." She flipped up, kissed Dad on the cheek, grabbed a plate, and forked a slice of French toast. "What time is it, A.M.?"

The rest of us were staring at our plates, not moving, but Devin either didn't notice or pretended not to. Anne Marie looked down at her watch and mumbled "Eight minutes."

"I WANT YOU TO HAVE A GOOD START TO YOUR DAY!" Dad screamed. "I mean it!" He slammed the spatula down on the table and stormed off toward the stairs, with Elvis, a blur of black Lab, right behind him. Dad tells on Colette to Mom, who thinks he should relax. We listened to him stomping up toward their bedroom.

"Well," said Devin. "And what a Good Start it is."

I tried not to smile because you just never know how Colette will react, but across the table, Bay cracked up. Anne Marie and Devin both started giggling, and when I dared look at Colette, there was a smile fighting its way onto her face, too.

"I'm not eating it," she said, struggling to stay serious.

"He didn't say you had to eat it," Anne Marie murmured.

"Yes, he did," said Bay.

"No." Anne Marie finished chewing and wiped her face on her napkin. "He said you're not going to school until that French toast is eaten."

"That's what he said," I agreed.

Bay stuck her fork into Colette's French toast and brought it over to her plate. She cut it, tossed half onto my newly emptied plate, and said, "Hurry."

"But I . . ."

Before I could finish saying I was totally stuffed on two huge pieces, Bay said, "Shut up and eat."

"Well, I'm not lying," said Colette.

"Why do you have to make such a *point* of it?" Devin asked. "Say what you need to, and get on with your life."

Colette looked at Anne Marie. We waited.

"Just avoid the question," Anne Marie said as she cleared her stuff into the kitchen. That seemed to settle it, pretty much. Anne Marie is like the junior mom of our house so she makes the rules; only Dad ever appeals her decisions to the real Mom.

I was shoving the last hunk of French toast into my mouth when Dad came storming down the stairs followed by Elvis and then Mom, who was holding an unplugged curling iron in her hair.

"Delicious!" Devin yelled, grabbing up her own plate and Colette's. "We made her eat it," she whispered to Mom.

"You ate?" Mom asked Colette. She released the curling iron and fluffed her hair a little.

Colette opened her mouth but Bay was faster. "Delicious, right, Colette?"

Mom and Dad looked at Colette. Anne Marie and Devin peered in from the kitchen. Bay and I held our breath. "I guess," Colette said. I finished chewing her last bite.

"Was it so bad?" Dad asked. He turned to Mom. "It took me five hours last night to make that barley bread. I made the Welsh barley bread, and . . ."

"Leave her alone, Arnie," Mom said. "She said she ate. Enough. Who even cares? What time is it? I have to be at work . . ."

"Seven forty-four. Gotta go," yelled Bay.

Mom headed toward the kitchen and threw her curling iron on the counter, mumbling, "Constant referee."

We all grabbed our lunches and kissed Dad. Well, Colette didn't. "Love you," Dad said to each of us, and then, "Come on, Elvis." He doesn't need to urge Elvis to come with him. Elvis is practically Dad's third foot.

"Don't forget your lunch!" Mom yelled after us. All five of us held up our brown bags as we scuffed down the back walk. She says don't forget your lunch instead of I love you.

On the way to the bus stop I felt like an elephant, so I lumbered behind with Colette. "I would've sat there all day," she said.

I could just see her sitting at the dining room table with her arms crossed when we got home. I shook my head. "I've never eaten so much French toast so fast in my life."

"I would've," Colette insisted.

"I believe you." I did, and I was too full to argue, anyway.

"I don't care if it's Welsh or not. I hate him."

I looked at her, stomping beside me. She's not much taller than I am and weighs ten pounds less. Since she showers at night, Colette was the only one of us with dry hair, and hers is the curliest. Like Dad's. She and Dad are a lot alike. I would never hate my father, as annoying as he can be. He's just Dad. I can't really see myself hating anybody. Not even Colette.

Her blue eyes, all outlined in black, looked so haunted and angry I almost asked her why she would do that to herself, but instead I said, "I like your eyeliner."

"Really?"

"Yeah," I lied.

She pushed her hair away from her face and asked, "Why don't you wear any makeup?"

I shrugged. "I think I'd feel too noticeable."

"Because you could be really pretty if you tried." She tucked my hair behind my ear.

"You think so?" I tucked back the other side.

She squinted at me. "Long blonde hair, the bluest eyes, high cheekbones — face it, Zoe. You're a dish."

"Please," I said, thinking, *Really?*

"You are," she said. "You know, you're my second favorite sister."

"I am?" That really surprised me. I thought she probably hated me, too.

She nodded.

I don't think she's my second favorite sister. She scares me. Besides, I wasn't sure whether or not to feel jealous that I only came in second. "Who's first?" I asked.

"He can't make me eat," she answered.

"Hey," I said. "What did you do yesterday? Devin wouldn't tell me. Is Devin your favorite?"

We were almost at the bus stop. She stopped and whispered, "It's a secret."

"I won't tell," I swore.

She stared me in the eyes for a few seconds. I thought, *Please, please.* Then she lifted her T-shirt to show her belly button. It had a very small gold hoop through it.

"Whoa," I said. "Did that hurt?"

"It kills. But I think it looks fierce, don't you?"

She didn't wait for me to answer because her boyfriend, Matt O'Donnell, yelled her name. He has the beginnings of a mustache and a ponytail. She skipped over to him and they started kissing hello.

Everybody watched. The high school bus pulled up

before they finished. They ended the kiss and smiled at each other. A twelfth-grade boy clapped; Matt bowed. He's sort of cute, I guess, in a grimy way. Even Colette has someone. Everybody but me trudged up the steps.

"You coming?" the driver asked me.

I realized I was just standing there spacing out. "No," I said. "I . . . I'm . . ." I was thinking it might be interesting to be Colette for a day and do only what I feel like doing, not worry about anybody else or how they're feeling. Be all jagged edges, make a point of things, run some panty hose, or whatever Anne Marie was saying. Let everybody else be careful of me, for a change. Pierce my belly button. Make out at the bus stop. Yeah, sure.

"She's just in seventh grade," Devin called from inside the bus.

"I'm big for my age," I explained.

"Oh," said the driver.

"Thanks," I said as she closed the door. I really do say thanks too much.

The bus pulled away. Bay and her best friend, Lauren, were waving at me out the back window. I waved back, wishing CJ were at my bus stop, or that Tommy and Jonas would show up already. I had nothing to do but wait, alone. I hate being left out.

## four

 "Don't the sixth graders look tiny?" CJ's best friend, Morgan, asked. "Can you believe we were that little last year?"

"I wasn't," I said.

"I still am," said Olivia Pogostin. She's four foot nine and sixty-seven pounds, which I find a bit hard to take at times, but she's really sincere and she has a pool table, so she's always been popular. She unlocked her locker with a key from her keychain. She's one quarter Filipino, one quarter black, and half white. The rest of us have combination locks and are just plain white.

"Wait for you by the wall," Tommy yelled, passing us.

"Great!" I yelled back.

Morgan blew her bangs away from her eyes and asked, "They're coming with us?"

"If that's OK," I said.

Nobody said anything for a minute. CJ and Morgan looked at each other.

"I could tell them forget it," I offered. "But what's the difference?"

"No," said Morgan. "That's fine with me."

"Me, too," agreed CJ.

"And maybe after," I suggested, "how about if we hang out at the pizza place?"

CJ smiled at me.

Morgan asked, "You like their pizza? It's so soggy."

"I don't care," I said.

"Sounds great to me," CJ whispered.

Olivia slammed her locker closed and said, "Have fun getting school supplies."

"Have fun at the orthodontist," I answered.

"That's likely. Hey, you three want to come over, after?" she asked. "I should be done by four-fifteen."

"Sounds good to me," I said. I love shooting pool. Morgan and CJ agreed, too. I noticed Tommy and Jonas weren't invited but I didn't say anything. I didn't want them to think I got boy-crazy over the summer or anything. Olivia thinks boy-crazy girls are pathetic.

"Wish me luck!" Olivia said, and ran toward the main door.

"Luck!" I yelled.

When Olivia was around the corner, CJ said, "My mom was saying Olivia thinks she might not have to get braces."

Morgan and I shook our heads. Everybody knew Olivia would be getting them. Her teeth are very crowded.

We headed out to meet the Levit boys by the wall. It was a relief to get outside on such a great day. It was so sunny and hot, Morgan and CJ had sat together under the chestnut tree at lunch instead of playing kickball. Olivia played, though, and Roxanne. I wasn't the only girl.

"Ready?" Morgan asked the boys. They jumped off the wall and we all started walking. She and CJ seemed perfectly happy to have Tommy and Jonas coming. I was glad. It's not like we're in fourth grade, afraid of cooties or something. No reason we can't all be friends.

Jonas asked Morgan, "Do you believe we have to sing 'Everything's Coming Up Roses' again this year?"

She laughed and blew her bangs away from her eyes. They're in chorus together, and they always make fun of the songs Mrs. Bauman chooses. They started walking really fast, inventing nasty new lyrics for the corny chorus songs. CJ and Tommy are in band with me, so we three walked together.

"Are we allowed to get erasable pens?" Tommy asked.

"I hate those," CJ said. "They leave smudges all over your hands."

"Yeah," said Tommy. "But you can change your mind." He kicked a rock. "Do you ever wear your hair down?"

CJ blushed and didn't answer. I jumped in for her, to help. "She looks awesome with it down."

"Because you always have it in a bun. It looks so tight." He was blushing, too. I've known him forever and this was the first time he blushed. He never blushed about my hair. Forget what Colette thinks — I obviously have boring hair.

{ 55 }

"It's for ballet," CJ said.

"But you're not doing ballet, right now," Tommy pointed out.

"It's big, down," CJ mumbled, touching it. We walked along a while without talking. I tried kicking a rock to Tommy. It was really heavy so I tripped. "Whoa," I said. They didn't say anything.

By the time we got into Sundries, Morgan and Jonas were already filling baskets. I took out my list and started collecting. When I was done, I went up to wait in line at the cash register. CJ was right behind me. She's pretty quick, too.

While we waited, we stared into the glass jewelry case beside us. "Which do you like?" CJ asked me in her quiet voice.

I pointed at a silver ring with a knot in it.

"Me, too," she whispered. We moved up a little. "Looks like a friendship ring, doesn't it?"

"Yeah," I whispered back. "Definitely. A friendship ring."

"Twenty-nine dollars," she said.

"They have installment." I casually pointed at the sign explaining the GREAT OPPORTUNITY NOW AVAILABLE: BUY IT ON THE INSTALLMENT PAYMENT PLAN! TAKE IT HOME TODAY! PAY IT OFF LATER!

"I get my allowance on Saturday," she said.

"Me, too." I'd dump my school supplies and buy rings with Mom's money instead, if CJ wanted. I could borrow paper.

"Looks like we'd need ten dollars each, for a down payment." She pointed at the small type on the sign. I nodded. So did she.

Morgan came up and stood between us. "Ooo, friend-ship rings," she whispered. "Which one do you like, CJ?"

CJ pointed at ours, the one with a knot.

"I knew it." Morgan smiled. "Good. Me, too."

"Great," said CJ.

I moved the bag of pens in my basket off the looseleaf because I didn't know what to do with myself.

"OK," CJ said, tapping me. "Your turn."

"Oh!" I quickly dumped all my stuff onto the counter.

The bag of pens slid over onto Mrs. Dodge's feet, behind the counter. "Sorry!" I stuffed my list into my pocket and tried to pull out the money Mom had given me, but my jeans were so tight I had a little trouble.

"Who's holding up the line?" Tommy yelled.

"Shut up, you," I yelled back.

I finally pulled myself together and paid, then waited outside, leaning against the ledge, for everybody else. Jonas was last. Tommy teased him the whole way to the pizza place about what a big deal he makes of every little decision.

"I don't want to end up with the wrong protractor," Jonas said, shrugging. He's a very serious person.

"Yeah," Tommy answered. "That could really wreck your year."

We pushed into the pizza place and headed for a booth toward the back. The boys got in first, then CJ sat down next to Tommy and Morgan sat down next to Jonas. There was no place left for me. I stood alone at the end of the table.

They all kept chatting. Nobody noticed there was only room in the booth for four. I smiled fakely and said, "Hi, my name is Zoe and I'll be your waitress?"

"You want to squish in here?" CJ asked. She scooched over a little. There might have been room for one cheek on that bench but no way my two.

"Nah. I'll get a chair," I said. I turned around and looked for one. I had to go all the way back to the front window and drag it screeching across the whole restaurant.

The waitress was standing where I had just been so I couldn't sit down yet. She turned to me and asked, "And you?"

I didn't know what anybody else had ordered. "A slice, please. Plain. And a ginger ale."

She left and I sat down. There was a pole where my legs wanted to be so I had to straddle it like I was riding a horse. "Everybody get good stuff?" I asked.

CJ nodded, then looked back at Tommy who was in the middle of telling us how he taught their little cousin Zachary all the different dinosaurs on Saturday.

I stood up and the chair scraped on the floor. The four of them looked up at me. "I'm just going to the bathroom," I said. My voice sounded so booming.

"I'll alert the media," said Tommy. I guess I wrecked his story.

"Ha." I meandered past the counter to the ladies' room. On my way into the stall, I closed the door too fast. My head was still out. I smashed it between the door and the stall wall. "Ow!" I said. Luckily nobody saw me. What a clod. Who smashes her own head in a door?

When I came out of the stall, after, Mrs. Dodge from Sundries was washing her hands next to me. She looked weird without the counter in front of her, separating us. She looked, I guess, vulnerable. Like I could knock her over too easily. Not that I would. Why would I knock down anybody, especially an old lady? I stared at myself to see if I looked on the outside like the wacko I felt like on the inside. Long blonde hair parted in the middle, pointy cheekbones and chin, blue eyes. Not a dish, not a wacko, just me — still totally recognizable, despite the bump above my right eye from the stall door.

"Do we please ourselves?" Mrs. Dodge asked me.

"Huh?" I think I said. I turned off the water and reached for a paper towel. Her eyes were gripped on mine in the mirror; I couldn't look away.

"What we see," she said. Then she left. I looked at myself in the mirror again. Please myself? I don't know. I sucked in my cheeks, which made me look more like Devin. I stuck out my tongue. Go light, Zoe, what's the matter with you lately? Must be the bump on my head.

When I got back to the table, there was a pitcher of 7UP and four plastic cups, and one can of ginger ale. "I didn't know we were getting a pitcher," I said. I opened my ginger ale and stuck in my straw. "Hey, the weirdest thing just happened."

But then the pizza came, and everybody was scrambling for the napkins and red pepper and garlic, so they weren't interested in my bathroom adventures. I straddled the table pole and gobbled down my soggy slice.

## five

When we got to her house, Olivia emptied a bag of potato chips into a big wooden bowl and we brought it downstairs.

"How did it go?" I asked Olivia.

"Don't ask," she said. "How about you?"

"Great," I said. But I noticed CJ and Morgan looked at each other and shrugged. I decided to shut up.

"You want to borrow some shorts?" Olivia asked me.

"Yeah, and put them on my what?"

"I have some big ones, or you could wear Dex's."

"Thanks anyway," I said. Dex is her gorgeous thirteen-year-old brother. His shorts probably would fit me. "I never get hot."

"Really?" asked Morgan. "I use deodorant, I sweat so much."

"Me, too," said CJ.

"You do?" I asked, with a mouth full of chips. "You look too innocent to need deodorant."

"I sweat buckets, dancing," CJ said. "You don't use it?"

"Yeah, I do," I said. "But . . ."

"Why should she?" Morgan interrupted. "If she never gets hot."

"Are we playing pool or talking about my armpits?" I asked. I hate being the topic.

We stood up and racked the balls and chose teams: me and CJ against Morgan and Olivia. Olivia was just trying to be nice, I know, offering me her brother's shorts, but sometimes she makes me feel like I bump into things.

Morgan scratched on the break. She was funny about it — she clonked her head on the table and asked to be taken out back and put out of her misery, she's so pathetic. I've always thought she was funny.

I shot next and sank the 2, so CJ and I got to be solids. I got the 4 in, too, then missed the 5. CJ said, "All right, partner."

That made me happy but I tried not to show it. "Please," I said.

Olivia made a really tough bank shot, but it's her table so she should be good. I decided not to worry. I'm pretty good, too.

"I stink," CJ said to me. "Don't be mad."

"I'm sure you're good," I assured her. I hoped I was right because Olivia sank the 14 in the corner pocket.

"That's OK," Morgan told CJ. "That evens out the teams, 'cause I stink worse." She blew her long bangs out of her eyes. Last year, her bangs were half an inch above her eyebrows. They look a lot better long, although she has to keep blowing at them.

"No way," said CJ. "You haven't seen me yet."

Olivia finally missed so it was CJ's turn. She barely tried. The cue ball popped off the table, sputtered, and didn't hit anything. CJ laughed. So did Morgan.

"You're right," Morgan said to her. "You stink."

They both cracked up.

I stopped myself from giving her a lesson on how to hold the cue the right way. "That's OK," I told her.

She and Morgan laughed even harder. Morgan hit next and by mistake knocked in the 5, which is a solid. She and CJ were holding each other, laughing so hard.

"Thanks," I said.

"Anytime," Morgan answered, blowing her bangs out of her eyes and shaking her head.

She left me lined up for an easy shot at the 7 in the side pocket. After I tapped it in, CJ stopped laughing and said, "Awesome." We high-fived. I peeked at Morgan, who glared back and then looked away. She stands with her feet farther apart than most people. It made me nervous, how angry she suddenly seemed.

"Yeah, but what am I gonna do now?" I asked, trying to get the laughing started again and be part of it this time.

Morgan pointed at the 3 and didn't smile back.

"Think so?" I was trying to be friendly.

Morgan slid her eyes past me to CJ and asked, "Do you think Jonas is getting funny-looking?"

"No," I answered. I walked around Morgan and lined up the 3 for a bank shot. "He looks the same." I didn't want her to be mad at me but Jonas is my friend. She shouldn't talk bad about him.

"He walks more and more like a chicken." Morgan imitated him and even I had to admit, it did look like both Jonas and a chicken. CJ laughed at that, which I didn't like. It felt like me and Jonas vs. CJ and Morgan, with Olivia neutral. Right when I was feeling psyched to be on CJ's team. I didn't know if I should try to laugh or not. I sort of wanted to go home.

"He's not as cute as Tommy, but he's really nice," CJ said. "Hard to believe they're twins."

"If you had to kiss one," asked Morgan, "which would you?"

I hit the 3 wide.

Olivia knocked in the 9 and said, "No interest."

"Hmmm," said CJ. "I guess I would kiss Tommy."

I pushed her. "No way," I said. "You like him? *Like* him, like him?"

Oh, no.

CJ explained, "She said if you *had* to. Who would you?"

Olivia came around to where I was standing. "Excuse me," she said. After I moved out of her way, she shot. The 15 teetered at the edge of the side pocket. She tried blowing but no luck.

"Well?" CJ asked me. "Which one would you kiss?"

"Your turn," I reminded her. What could I say, when she just chose Tommy? Let's shoot it out for who gets him?

While she bent over the table lining up an impossible shot, I said, "They're both my friends." That's what I always say. I think it's still true.

"Oh," CJ said. She missed badly, then turned to Morgan and asked, "Who would you kiss?"

"Neither," said Morgan, who was practically lying on the table to reach the cue ball. "I hate them both." She missed, too.

CJ balanced on her cue and arabesqued toward Morgan. "If somebody put a gun to your head?"

"Yours," Olivia said to me. I found an angle on the 3 and sunk it. I got in the next two, then called the 8 in the far side pocket and sunk that, too.

"On fire!" Morgan said, even though she had just lost. You could see why CJ chose her as a best friend — she's a good sport. When I fixed her up with Tommy last year, he said, "Yeah, all right, she's a good sport." That's what I've always liked about her. I've always liked her.

"Lucky shots," I said, trying to be a good sport, too. I wanted to tell them how I had lined up that last shot, but nobody likes a gloater, so I held it in, and we all went upstairs for some ice cream.

CJ slid gracefully into a chair and sat with her skinny legs straddled. She does that for ballet, she had told me the morning after I slept over — ballet dancers have to push their knees apart all the time, to improve turn-out. I stopped myself from explaining to Morgan and Olivia why CJ sits like that. Morgan probably already knew what turn-out is, from being best friends with CJ since fourth grade.

My hip caught on the arm of my chair as I tried to sit down. It tipped, but I caught it before it fell over. I plopped down hard, trying to make my cloddishness look intentional. "Call me Grace," I joked.

"You OK?" CJ asked.

"Great," I said. *Just thinking about kissing at the bus stop,* I thought. *Just trying to avoid Morgan's eyes.*

Olivia placed bowls of Cookies 'N Creme in front of each of us. I dug right in before I noticed Morgan and CJ were waiting for Olivia to sit down. I tried to swallow the glob of ice cream whole so they wouldn't see me chew. I got a burning ice-cream neckache from it.

Morgan tipped back in her chair and said, "I think that was really selfish of the boys, don't you?"

"What?" I tried to rub my throat without their noticing.

"They didn't even ask their mother to give us a ride here?"

"It's right down the street," CJ said.

"Still," said Morgan. She took a large spoonful, which I was happy to see, but then she just licked it as if it were a cone.

"I guess they could've asked," CJ agreed.

Olivia stood up to get the dish of sprinkles. With her back turned, she mumbled, "You're just still upset about the kiss."

"Well, Tommy is a horn-dog," said Morgan.

We all laughed.

"How hard did he kiss you, anyway?" Olivia asked.

"Hard," said Morgan. "But I dumped him for it and I'm over the jaw pain. It's been seven months. I'm just saying, I think it would've been nice . . ."

"It would've," Olivia agreed. "Who wants more sprinkles?"

"I do," I said. Nobody else asked for more. I hunched down a little in my chair.

"Well," said Morgan, blowing the bangs out of her dark eyes again. "I say we teach them some manners."

"How?" asked CJ.

"S.T.," Morgan whispered.

Olivia leaned forward. "What's that?"

"Silent Treatment. Let them figure out why we're not talking to them, and maybe they'll learn, for next time."

"What if they talk to us?" I asked. "I mean, they're on my bus."

"Don't do it if you don't want to," Morgan said, frowning. "But it will only work if we stick together."

Olivia shrugged. "I'm not even friends with them, really."

"That's not the point," said CJ.

"I didn't say it was," Olivia snapped back. Their mothers are best friends. Sometimes Olivia and CJ are very close, like when they come back from being on vacation together, but other times they bicker like Anne Marie and Bay used to. They know too many details about each other's families.

"Well, I'll do it," CJ said, and looked at me. I wasn't mad at the boys, and they're my friends. CJ tilted her head a little to the side, the way she had when she looked at the rings in the display case at Sundries. She was waiting to see if I would be willing to join her. Morgan was.

I put a half-eaten spoonful back into the green bowl and said, "OK, I'll do it."

A horn beeped — it was CJ's mom, there to pick us up already. Olivia's mom ran out from her study and bent into the car window, her long black hair in a braid down her back. We weren't finished eating but we had to throw the bowls quickly into the sink. Too bad, because the ice cream was delicious, and the truth is, I do get hot. I was just saying that to avoid an older brother's shorts.

"Did you have fun?" Mrs. Hurley asked as the three of us settled into the backseat and waved to Olivia.

"Yeah," said CJ. "'Bye, Auntie Betsy!" She blew a kiss to Mrs. Pogostin. They're not really related, just family friends. Maybe I could call Mrs. Levit *Auntie Joan*. Ha, ha.

As she was pulling into the street, Mrs. Hurley asked, "So? Did you have fun? What did you do?" My mother never asks that. She just asks if I said thank you.

"Nothing," CJ said, just as I was about to blurt out our entire afternoon. *It was so nice of her to ask,* I thought.

"Sounds like fun," said Mrs. Hurley. "How was Olivia's appointment?"

CJ shrugged. "We got school supplies and played pool," she said. "Zoe was awesome, and Olivia, of course. I stank."

"So did I," said Morgan. They smiled at each other.

"No you didn't," I said. "They were fine."

Mrs. Hurley pulled into my driveway. I got out. It makes sense that she would drop me off first — I live closest to Olivia, and Morgan lives practically down the street from CJ — but I still felt bad. Left out.

"Don't forget," Morgan reminded me. She put her finger over her thin lips. "S.T."

"I won't forget."

"I'll call you tonight," CJ said.

"Great," I answered. I wasn't sure what we would talk about since we just spent the whole day together but I was happy she wanted to. I waved as Mrs. Hurley backed down my driveway. CJ waved back, but Morgan looked away, out her window.

# six

fter dinner, CJ called. I tried
to think of a funny story to tell her. In the back of my
mind I was thinking I should probably just relax and let
CJ tell me a funny story for once, but it feels so good to
make her laugh I wanted to prepare something.

"Guess what happened at dinner?" I said.

"What?"

I couldn't think of anything to say. I was hoping something would pop into my head, but it didn't. Nothing had
happened at dinner, nothing special, nothing interesting,
we all just ate as fast as we could, which is what always
happens at my house, because if you eat slow, you don't

get seconds. I listened to the silence of CJ waiting to hear what happened at my dinner, and the more I didn't say anything, the more I couldn't think of any way out.

"We ate."

"You what?" CJ laughed.

"Dad made pasta with meatballs and we ate it. It was the most boring dinner I ever had." This was not the truth, but I felt like I should spice it up somehow. There have probably been even more boring dinners at my house — I just didn't necessarily remember them, because they were so boring. "I mean," I said, hoping I'd come up with something midsentence, "the first day of school. You'd think something interesting would come up over dinner. Especially since it's our last first day all together, because next year Anne Marie will be gone."

"Oh, Zoe," she said in that slow way of hers. "That's right. Are you depressed?"

"No," I said. Depressed is a word I've never thought of in relation to myself. Everything is always fine with me. Only Colette gets depressed in my family. But then again, maybe I did feel a little blue. I didn't think I was allowed. "Maybe."

"Yeah, I know what you mean," CJ said.

"Why? Are you depressed, too?" I kneeled on the couch and looked out into the side yard at the tree that had a broken old swing hanging from a branch. It was moving a tiny bit, like it was hoping to be noticed and played with.

"No," she said, and then, "Maybe."

"Why?"

"I don't know."

"Is it about dance?" I whispered. "What you told me?"

"No." You could hear the period at the end of that no.

I tried to think what could be bothering her. "It's not because of pool today, is it? Because you just need practice."

"No, I don't care about pool."

I squinted out the window, trying to see if the branch had grown all the way over the swing's rope. "Oh," I said. I couldn't really see. It was too dark.

"What in the world is that?" Dad yelled from the kitchen.

"Nothing!" I heard Colette yell back.

"Is there something sticking through your skin?"

"Oh, man," I whispered.

"Do you think my hair is disgusting?" CJ asked.

"Um," I said. I wasn't paying attention, to be honest. Daddy had stormed out of the kitchen, screaming up the steps for Mom.

"You do," CJ said. "You think my hair is disgusting."

"No," I whispered. "You have great hair. It's always so perfect, with a style and everything." It was getting dark enough for me to see my reflection in the window. I touched my own long, boring hair. "Mine hangs smooshed against my head, blah."

"You could put yours up," she suggested. I was just saying that. I actually always until that minute thought it looked good, hanging blah. "Or not," she added when I didn't answer.

I watched Mom come clattering down the stairs. She grabbed Colette's shirt and pulled it up to reveal the little gold hoop.

"What is wrong with this child?" Dad screamed. "Get this girl to a psychiatrist; she has gone totally insane!"

"Oh, Colette," sighed Mom. "That looks ridiculous."

Dad's neck veins bulged. "What do you think you're doing?"

"Nothing. I pierced my belly button," Colette answered quietly.

"What's going on there?" CJ asked me.

"Hold on."

"And you're encouraging her?" Mom asked Anne Marie.

Poor Anne Marie was caught between them, holding a bottle of alcohol and a cotton ball. "It could get infected," she said.

Mom shrugged at Daddy and said, "It's a stage."

"Take it out," Daddy told Colette.

"No." Colette pulled her shirt back down over her stomach. "It's my body."

"Not while it lives in my house, it's not!" Dad screamed.

"Zoe?" CJ asked. "Is somebody screaming there?"

"One sec."

Mom was pointing up the stairs. "Colette? Upstairs."

Dad yelled after her, "And that thing better be off your body by tomorrow! I mean it!"

Colette loves being sent to her room. She told me so this summer. In there she doesn't have to deal with anybody but Bay, who doesn't bother her much. Bay must be her favorite, I guess.

When Colette's door slammed, Mom said, "That one is going to be the death of me." She sounded a little amused.

"It is her body," Anne Marie tried tentatively.

"Don't you start," Mom warned her.

Dad stomped out to the backyard. He has a cigarette out there sometimes, though he swears he quit. I've seen the ashes.

"Anyway," I whispered to CJ.

"Was I on hold?" No laugh in her voice. She did sound depressed.

"Sorry." I tried to think quick what to do. Mom says you don't hang your dirty laundry out for the neighbors to see, so I can't tell people bad stuff about my family. I said, "That was pretty rude of Tommy and Jonas today, huh?"

"You think?" CJ asked. "Morgan said she wasn't sure if you agreed."

"I did."

"I told her so," CJ said.

"Thanks." So I guess she and Morgan had already talked. Well, what did I expect? Morgan is her best friend.

"And when Tommy said that thing about my bun?"

"I don't think he meant anything bad," I told her.

"Yeah, well, now he got me all depressed about my hair."

"You have great hair," I said again.

"Right," she said. "I have to wear a bun or my hair takes over the classroom. No one can fit in a stairwell with me if it's not up. And Tommy made me feel terrible about it."

"He just . . ."

"Are you on his side?"

"No," I said.

"You sound like you're on his side," CJ whispered.

"I'm not," I assured her.

"You don't like him, do you?"

*If you only knew.* "No!" I insisted. "Please."

Neither of us talked for a few seconds. I should've said *Yeah, maybe I do.* If I want to be best friends, I should tell her my secrets. But I couldn't tell her, not the way she asked, like it would be a total betrayal of her if I did. My lie just hung there and I listened to it.

"Hey," CJ said finally. "What did you think about those rings today?"

"Nice."

"Mmm," she hummed.

I couldn't help saying, "Morgan liked the same one, huh?"

"Yeah. That was funny."

"Really," I said. Oh, hilarious.

"I never had a friendship ring with anybody," CJ whispered.

"Not even Morgan?"

"No."

"Me, neither," I answered. "I mean, obviously I never had one with Morgan."

"Right."

"Why would I? When she's your best friend."

"Yeah. Anyway, good luck with the S.T. tomorrow."

"I just meant I never had one with anybody, either," I said, and hung up. "But," I added, "I guess you probably figured that out."

## seven

At the bus stop the next morning, while I was busy trying to give him the Silent Treatment, Jonas asked, "So what do you think about that thing Madame F said?"

I didn't answer him. I looked away, up the street.

"Yesterday," he said.

I felt ridiculous but I kept not answering. I never gave anyone a Silent Treatment before. It's hard.

"In French class?" he added, as if I just needed clarification.

I couldn't let him think I was a total idiot. "Which

thing?" I asked casually, as if there were lots of things she said that I understood and had opinions about.

"You know, that she takes a quarter point off your final grade every time you miss a homework?"

I totally missed that. "Pretty harsh," I said, then looked away again. *Stop talking to him,* I reminded myself. *Teach him a lesson, or whatever.*

"So, did you do the homework?" he asked.

I started whistling.

"That's what I thought," Jonas said. "Which ones do you need?"

"That's OK," I said, still looking away from him. The bus was late. So was Tommy. Jonas and I were alone. Who would know if I talked to him? But I wanted to be true to Morgan and Olivia and especially CJ.

"I don't mind," he assured me. He held out his neat paper. I think he copies over his work. What a dweeb. I looked at him. He has the happiest face, rosy cheeks and long eyelashes. He'd gotten a haircut since I saw him yesterday, and his curls were standing up a little in the back. He's cute, too, I realized, but I don't get a jiggly nervous feeling being with him. Just buddies, like I used to feel with Tommy.

"No," I said.

He slipped his homework back into one of his new folders. We stood there not talking for a few minutes.

Tommy ran up and said, "Whoa, thought I was screwed."

I peeked at him, then looked away quick.

"Something's wrong with Zoe," Jonas said.

"What?"

"I don't know."

"What's wrong with you?" Tommy asked me.

I burst out laughing. "Shut up," I said. "There's nothing wrong with me."

"She says there's nothing wrong," Tommy told Jonas.

I was feeling pretty stupid. I kept squinting up the street.

"I don't know," Jonas said. "I guess she's really interested in where the bus is."

I cracked up again. "You guys."

"What?"

I turned around and saw them both with these super-innocent looks on their faces. I dropped my books and shoved each of them with one hand. Tommy dropped his books, too, ready to really get into it. I held up my hand. I was wearing Anne Marie's big yellow cotton top, and she'd kill me if I grass-stained it, wrestling him. And I don't need him thinking I'm a guy. Where does that get me?

"It just would've been nice if you guys had offered us a ride to Olivia's."

"What?" asked Tommy.

The bus lurched into sight. "Yesterday," I said.

"If you wanted a ride you should've asked," Jonas said. "We were just going to the barber. Our mother wouldn't care."

He was right. Mrs. Levit is pretty good about giving people rides. She likes to have people to tell her private life to.

"Yeah, but . . ." I said. "And Tommy teased CJ about her bun?"

The doors creaked open. Jonas climbed in first, and Tommy followed me, poking my shoulder. "I didn't tease her about it. I asked her about it." He slid into a seat next to Lou Hochstetter.

I had no answer to that.

"Nice haircut," I said. I sat across the aisle, next to Jonas.

"Nice knee," Tommy answered.

"Thanks." I smiled at him, trying to keep my gums hidden so I'd be cuter, and pushed my knee against the seat in front so nobody would see how wrecked it looked anymore. Maybe he meant it, that my knee looked nice, I tried telling myself. That's unlikely, for sure, but I sort of meant it about his haircut, so maybe there was a chance. I glanced at him. He was drumming on his notebook, looking out the window. It was a nice haircut. Very nice. Youch.

## eight

Good thing I wore shorts, despite my scab — the second day of school was starting out even hotter than the first. I sweated silently the rest of the bus ride. When we finally pulled into the circle, CJ and Morgan were sitting on the wall together, waiting for the bell. The most popular seventh graders last year sat there every morning. I bolted toward them, glad to get away from the boys.

Mrs. Pogostin dropped off Olivia and Dex. We waved to Olivia, who sprinted over. Dex joined a game of keep-away with a bunch of other eighth-grade guys. Part of me thought I'd like to play, too — I'm pretty good at keep-away because I'm tall, but I wasn't going to be the only girl. I'm learning. Olivia couldn't make it up the wall, so I jumped down to give her a boost, then climbed back up myself. When Mr. Luse dropped Roxanne off, she ran over, too, pressing her glasses to the bridge of her nose.

The first bell rang and the kids who get free lunch rushed inside because before school they get a muffin or something from the cafeteria. None of us did. We could take our time.

"Did you do the French?" Roxanne asked me.

"No," I admitted. "Did you?"

She nodded. "She scared me. You want it?" She almost dropped her books, trying to yank her blotchy paper out of her loose-leaf.

"Thanks." I quick started copying her work, feeling really happy I hadn't betrayed my girlfriends by talking to Jonas. While I wrote, I shook my head and said, "A quarter point for each homework?"

"I know it," said Roxanne. "Oops." Her loose-leaf got away from her and exploded when it hit the ground. She jumped down and chased after the blowing papers. CJ jumped down, too, and helped her. I would've but I had to hurry.

"I hope you remember French from last year," I yelled down to her. "I want to get a good mark. I take a lot of pride in my work."

"Oh, yeah," said Roxanne, stomping on the last couple of loose pages. "Me, too. A lot of pride." She plopped down on the ground to rest. "Too bad Miss Marcus is gone."

"I loved her," I agreed. Miss Marcus was our French teacher last year. She was twenty-three and couldn't control us at all. "We didn't learn anything." I closed my notebook.

"Zoe?" Morgan whispered to me. "How was it?"

"How was what?" I grabbed CJ's hand to help her back up.

On the other side of me, Morgan whispered, "This morning?"

"No problem," I lied. The warning bell rang so I tossed my lunch and backpack down from the wall. CJ's quilted bag landed at the same time I did.

"Thanks," I said to Roxanne, handing her back her homework.

She shoved it into her notebook and, heading into school, said, "No biggie." Some people say Roxanne is a mess, but I think she's fun.

Morgan threw down her bag, and she and CJ jumped

together, kicking their legs out. Olivia turned backward and slid carefully down the wall. I had started toward the entrance when CJ said, "Zoe?"

"Yeah?"

"Could you grab my lunch for me? I forgot it." Her hair wasn't in a bun for the first time ever at school. It was puffy and soft like the night I had slept over. She kept smooshing it down.

"Mine, too?" asked Morgan.

I looked up at the two slightly crumpled brown bags slumping on top of the wall.

"Can you reach?" CJ asked. "I'm too short."

"Me, too," said Morgan.

I hesitated. Did they leave their lunches up there on purpose to make a point? That they are best friends, or that they are little and I am a big clod like Roxanne?

Morgan isn't that much shorter than I am, now that she grew over the summer. What right did she have to call me tall?

"Sure," I said and grabbed their lunches, telling myself to quit being a paranoid nut.

"Thanks," they said together. *How cute of them,* I thought nastily. We went to our lockers to throw in our lunches.

"OK," I said to everybody, slamming mine shut. "See you second."

"See ya," said Morgan.

"See ya," said CJ. She smooshed her hair again. I almost told her don't worry, it looks fine, but I didn't feel like it. Let Morgan tell her.

We split up to go to homeroom. Olivia and I both have

Ms. Masters, the nurse, for homeroom, so we walked together. I didn't chat on the way like I normally would.

"Can you keep a secret?" she asked.

"Sure," I said, not even psyched.

"I'm getting braces."

"Really?" I wasn't quite listening. I was too busy calling myself tall: *You are so TALL, you big TALL, would you get our lunches, you horrifyingly TALL?* I don't think I was very sympathetic to poor Olivia.

As I sat down at my spot at Ms. Masters's table, it occurred to me that this was the closest I'd ever come to crying in school and that maybe Devin wasn't crazy. Maybe my hormones were kicking in. I ran my hand over my face to check for a sudden outbreak of pimples.

After the Pledge was done, the bell rang.

"Don't tell anybody," Olivia said as she left for Spanish.

"I won't."

I was slumped behind my desk, concentrating on trying to feel my hormones, when Madame F said something final-sounding. I looked around to see what everybody else would do in response. I guess she'd said, Roxanne and Bernadette, please come up to the front and hand out these big ugly textbooks, because that's what happened. While they were passing out the books and I was feeling lucky that she hadn't asked me to, I heard the one word I'd been dreading most.

"Zoe?"

I looked up. I couldn't remember a single word in French. Like the word for "here" or "what" or "yes" or anything. I tried to look at her with an encouraging expression, like, yes, go on, I'm listening.

"(Something in French)?" Madame F asked. Sweat attack. I tried desperately to remember a word, any word, and just say it in hopes it would answer what she asked.

"No." I tried to say it in a French-y way.

*"Non?"* she asked, in her perfect French accent. She looked puzzled. So obviously *no* wasn't working for her. I glanced over at Jonas. He was pointing to his paper. I looked back at Madame F. She was staring at me. I couldn't take a chance. Just then Roxanne dropped a textbook. *I love her,* I decided, big clod or not. When Madame F flicked her eyes to the back of the room to look, I quickly focused on Jonas's paper. It said 12.

"Twelve," I said quickly. Then I thought, *Oh, I guess she*

*asked how old I am.* "No" would be a pretty ridiculous answer to that. I started to smile.

*"En français,"* said Madame F.

"Um," I said and then something popped into my head. "Dues," I said hopefully.

*"J'ai douze ans, madame,"* she said. Everything she says sounds like delicious food. I tried to repeat her words. I guess I came close enough because she moved on to torture Lou Hochstetter. I was impressed with myself that I came up with anything at all.

I smiled at Jonas and he smiled back. He has very red lips. My stomach rumbled. *Go light,* I told myself. *You're not even supposed to be feeling friendly toward him.*

## nine

I looked down at my palm to read my combination, which I had written there in Bic. "It takes my brain a while to get back into gear after the summer," I explained. "Seven-fourteen-two."

"That's easy," Olivia said. "Just remember seven goes into fourteen twice."

"Announce it, why don't you," said CJ.

"Nobody heard," Olivia argued.

I shrugged. "Not that I have anything valuable."

CJ smooshed her hair down again and tucked it behind her ears.

I looked at Morgan, but Morgan didn't reassure her, so I told CJ, "Don't worry. It looks fine."

"Really?" CJ smiled. "I can't believe I wore it down. It feels so . . . large."

I laughed. "I like large hair."

"You do?"

"Yeah."

"Thanks." CJ wrote something on her assignment pad, tore off the paper, folded it, and handed to me. "Here's my combination," she explained. "In case I'm sick or something, so you can get my stuff for me."

"OK." I pushed the note into my pocket. "And I guess you all have mine, now." Morgan and Olivia nodded but kept looking deep into their lockers. CJ hadn't given her combination to either of them.

Morgan slammed her locker and said, "Well, my dad is at it again."

"Oh, no," CJ said. She shook her head sadly.

"What?" I asked. I hate not knowing.

"You wouldn't understand, Zoe," Morgan said. "You have the perfect family." She wrote down her combination and held it out to Olivia. "Here's mine," she said.

"Thanks," said Olivia. She looked surprised.

CJ slammed her locker shut and fiddled with the combination.

I told Morgan, "My family is so far from perfect."

"Excuse me?" Morgan leaned against Olivia's locker. "The Grandons? You're all so happy and friendly and cute, we could throw up."

"Mm-hmm," CJ agreed, without looking up. "Everybody thinks so." They both nodded, in unison, then smiled at each other. I put my hand in my pocket to feel CJ's combination. She gave it to *me*.

"My family?" I asked. "Please." I never thought of us as cute, except maybe Devin. I wondered if they included me in that.

Morgan blew her long brown bangs out of her eyes. "You have no problems, Zoe, face it."

"Sure," I said. "So, what did your dad do?"

"Oh, he called last night with a whole thing why there won't be a check again this month. My mother went nuts. And she says I have a nasty mouth."

We headed down the hall toward the cafeteria. CJ reached her arm up around Morgan.

"My family isn't so perfect, either, you know," I said. We crossed to a table near the back of the cafeteria.

"Right," said Morgan.

We all stepped into the benches and pulled our sandwiches out. I didn't really want to show my dirty laundry, but I felt like we were all chipping in for something and I hadn't paid my share yet. Also, OK, maybe I had to top Morgan.

"My sister Colette got her belly button pierced, and my dad saw it."

CJ turned toward me. "Did he have a fit?"

"Oh, yeah," I said. "When I was on the phone with you? That was him, screaming that she better have it out by today, and she's screaming no way, it's her body, he can't make her, and he's like, oh, yes I can. CJ was on the phone with me the whole time."

"That's true," CJ told Morgan and Olivia, with her green eyes open wide. "I heard the whole thing."

Olivia opened her pretzel sticks and said, "I agree with your sister. Even though, gross, still, it's her body."

"Maybe," said Morgan, taking a pretzel. "But she doesn't have to make such a dramatic point of it."

I shrugged. "That's what my sister Devin says. I don't know. But anyway, my family is far from perfect, is the point."

Just as Tommy and Jonas came over and sat down, CJ said, "You must be so upset."

"Why?" Tommy asked, shaking his milk. "What happened?"

"Nothing," said Morgan.

I ducked my head. I didn't want to get myself in trouble or have anyone think I was on the boys' side or liked one of them. CJ put her arm protectively around me.

"OK," said Tommy, shrugging.

Jonas grabbed a few of Olivia's pretzel sticks and said, "Yum," as he bit the tops off.

"You could ask," Morgan snapped.

Jonas stopped chewing. He lowered the bottom halves of the pretzel sticks back into Olivia's box and mumbled, "Sorry."

He and Tommy stood up.

"Later," said Tommy as they walked away.

"Much," I said.

My friends laughed. I felt bad, but what could I do? Luckily, Tommy wouldn't be mad at me for that. He doesn't care.

"Do you think she'll take it out?" Olivia asked me. "The earring? The belly button ring? Whatever you call it."

I shook my head slowly.

"Is he really going to check, you think?" Morgan asked.

I nodded. "Tonight. Should be a comedy."

CJ rubbed my back. "If you need to get away," she suggested, "just call me. You can come over."

"Thanks," I said.

"Or me," Morgan offered. "Anytime."

"My house is closest," Olivia said. "You can ride your bike over if you want."

I smiled at them. It felt really good, knowing they were behind me. Sometimes it's easier being with my friends than with my family. They understand me more, don't just think of me as The Baby. They have time for me.

"You guys are the best," I said. I was happy I told

them, even though my mother would have my head if she knew. Family business stays in the family.

Tommy threw a handful of minimarshmallows at us. We decided to eat them instead of throwing them back.

## ten

I was expecting CJ. I picked up the phone after Devin yelled it was for me and said, "Hey, CJ!" But it was Morgan.

"Zoe?" she asked.

"Morgan?"

"Yeah," she said. "Did you think CJ was calling you?"

"No, I . . . never mind. What's up?" I pushed my hair behind my ears and looked at my reflection in the window. It wasn't any prettier than the normal way. Maybe a little more sophisticated, though.

"I was just wondering if you got the math homework," she said. "I forgot to write down the pages."

"Oh, sure," I told her. "Hold on." I ran up and got my assignment pad and read it off to her.

"Did you do it yet?" she asked.

"No," I said.

"Me, neither."

We did the homework over the phone together. I love doing homework over the phone; it's so much less boring that way. About halfway through, Morgan asked, "Do you think we were a little harsh on the boys?"

"I don't know." I thought it might be a trick question. There's something about Morgan I don't one hundred percent trust. Maybe because she keeps blowing at her hair lately. It makes me nervous. Or maybe because I'm trying to steal her best friend.

"They seemed really upset," she said.

I put down my pen and turned backward on the couch to look through my reflection out at the tree — my favorite talking-on-the-phone position. "Um," I said.

"Yeah. They did."

"I think we should end the S.T. What do you think?"

"OK."

"Their haircuts look sort of cute," she added. "Don't you think?"

"I didn't notice."

"Oh," she said.

*If you only knew,* I thought. *I spent all day noticing their haircuts.* But I didn't want anybody to know I'd been thinking about the Levits more than usual. It's just too weird.

"Anyway," Morgan whispered. "Did your dad check Colette?"

"He's not home from the bakery yet," I told her. "Thursday is his late night. But she still has it in there, she showed me."

"Are you a wreck?"

"Yeah." Although I appreciated her support, I really hate talking about stuff nobody should know. What if my mother picked up? I'd be dead. So I asked, "How was gym?" She has gym while I'm in band, eighth period.

"Oh, it stunk. Gymnastics."

"I hate gymnastics," I said. "I feel like such a clod."

"Well, next to CJ, we all do," said Morgan.

Talking with her about CJ made me a little tense.

"Please," I answered. "She can do a split and rest her head in the middle."

"I know," Morgan said. "She learned that in fourth grade."

"I know," I said back, not wanting to lose the who-knows-CJ-better competition.

"You're doing soccer, right?" she asked me.

I was so relieved to be on a normal topic, I said, "Absolutely!"

"I guess I am, too," she said. "But I don't really care that much about it because I want to concentrate on soft-ball. Don't you?"

"I like both," I said. Morgan didn't make starter last year in soccer; I knew she felt bad about that, no matter how much she denied it.

"With you pitching, I definitely think we've got a shot

at regionals this year, in softball, if we focus," Morgan said. "What did you strike out — seven in that final game last year?"

"I don't remember, maybe six," I said. It was eight. I remembered every pitch.

"What a game, huh? That ugly girl I thought was gonna cry."

"Really?" I asked, feeling happy. "Well, you were great at First."

"Thanks. I was thinking, though," Morgan said, quieter. "Just between us. Maybe it's good that CJ will be too busy with dance this year to play. Because, no offense, I mean she's my best friend, but she has no arm."

"I know," I admitted. I felt a little guilty talking about CJ that way, but Morgan was right. CJ is not great at sports.

We talked softball a little more, and some about soccer, which starts next week, before we finished the homework. When we were done, Morgan thanked me and
said, "Don't say anything to CJ, about what I said."

"I won't," I assured her. "And I definitely think you'll
start in soccer. You're probably faster, now that you grew."

"Whatever," said Morgan. "Maybe you could come
over sometime next week and we can have a catch or
something."

"OK," I said. "That sounds great." I hung up and
called CJ right away.

"Did you hear about the Silent Treatment?" I asked
when she picked up.

"What about it?" She recognized my voice.

"Morgan just called for the math homework. We got
to talking and she canceled it. She felt really bad, I think.

About today. She thinks we maybe overdid it." I was picturing going over to Morgan's to play catch. I liked it that she thought I almost made that ugly girl cry. It was great to have had such a normal conversation. I felt like regular old Zoe again for the first time since Labor Day.

CJ asked, "She called you for the math homework?"

"Yeah," I said. I was pacing around the living room, mentally replaying last year's final game.

"I can't believe her," CJ said.

"You mean that she'd call me of all people for the math homework?" I asked. "Thanks a lot."

"No," CJ protested. "Not that —"

"I think she regretted the Silent Treatment thing," I interrupted, not needing her to apologize. I knew really she was probably upset that Morgan hadn't called her, since they're best friends. Sometimes I misunderstand on purpose.

"No," CJ said again. "I mean, she did the math homework over the phone with me an hour ago."

The game clicked off in my head. I stopped pacing. "You're kidding."

"I'm totally, totally serious," CJ answered.

"That's too weird." I kneeled backward on the couch to sort this out but I got distracted by the swing. Nobody has used it in a really long time. Tommy and Jonas and I used to have contests of who could jump farthest off it. I guess we're all too old for that, now. That's what I was thinking about instead of Morgan.

"She's probably on with Olivia right now, doing the math again," CJ said. "I can't believe her."

"Actually, I bet she called Olivia first, to get the right answers." I laughed. "At least now I don't feel so stupid!"

"You know what we should do?" CJ asked.

"What?" I asked.

Colette came down and stood in front of me with her hands on her hips. "I need the phone."

"We should call her," CJ interrupted.

"Who? Olivia?" I asked.

"No. Morgan," CJ said. "I have three-way calling."

"I have to tell Matt something," Colette insisted.

"In a minute," I said to Colette. She shook her head but went away. "What's three-way calling?" I asked CJ.

"You can be on the line secretly while I call Morgan back to ask if she's spoken to you, and see if she lies, and catch her."

I said, "OK." Don't be nervous, I told myself — it's just a prank. I'm not the one about to be caught. Why should I worry?

As CJ dialed, I listened to Anne Marie drilling Bay on SAT vocabulary words in the dining room. They were cracking up because Devin had just come in and given a disgusting definition of the word *pulchritude*. When it's time for me to take the SATs, nobody will live here anymore but my parents.

On the second ring, CJ told me to stop breathing so loud. I flipped the mouthpiece over my head and covered it with my hand.

They chatted for a minute before CJ asked Morgan if she had spoken to me tonight. I held my breath.

"No," Morgan said. "Why?"

"Just wondering," said CJ.

*Gotcha*, I thought. Like the FBI was about to burst into her kitchen and arrest her for it. Devin shuffled past me to the den and said, "Your pulchritude is showing." I put my finger to my lips and yanked my shorts a little lower in case pulchritude meant fat thighs.

"I feel so bad for Zoe," Morgan was telling CJ, meanwhile.

Oh, dread. I settled into the couch to hear why.

"For Zoe?" CJ asked.

"Yeah," Morgan said. "She is such a nice girl. Everybody loves her. But it's like, all she ever wants to talk about is sports."

"Ummm," said CJ.

I stopped myself from pointing out that she's the one who brought up softball, not me. I thought she wanted to talk about it.

"I guess mostly I just feel bad about the boy-thing," Morgan said. "You know, like we were saying last night."

I bit on my cheeks and kept the talk-part of the phone covered above my head. My heart was pounding really fast. *What were you saying last night, CJ?*

"Morgan . . ." CJ's voice sounded a little shaky.

"You know, about the boys not liking her in that way."

"I didn't say that." CJ didn't sound so sure. "I don't know who the boys like."

"Come on," said Morgan. "You know who they *don't* like."

I swallowed and sank deeper into the couch.

So boys don't like me in that way. No big deal. Tommy and I will always be just friends. Obviously. I know who the boys *don't* like. It's not like I've never realized.

"Ummm," said CJ. "I gotta go."

"Don't say anything to Zoe," Morgan said before she hung up. I slipped onto the floor and thought, *Oh, yeah, CJ? Well, you have no arm! Don't think I'm the only one people talk about behind her back! You should hear what we were saying about you!*

"I didn't say that," CJ said as soon as she cleared off the second line.

"Hey, it's the truth," I admitted.

"It is not!" CJ said.

"I know I'm not pretty. No need to alert the media." I tried to laugh but it came out like pathetic gasps for air instead.

"Well, if the boys only like girls who are so pretty, then, forget it — that's just, stupid, stupid, stupid."

She didn't say, *Oh, no, Zoe — you are pretty, really pretty.* Not that I expected her to. "Stupid," I mumbled.

"And Morgan is a . . . I can't even trust her. I can't believe she used to be my best friend."

"Used to be?"

Dad's headlights lit up the window as his car pulled
into the driveway.

"We're just very different," CJ said. "Morgan doesn't
understand about, you know, anything, I told you, before. And now I can't even, I mean, like, *you* would never
talk about somebody behind her back. Right?"

"Well . . . I gotta go," I whispered. "My dad's on his way
in."

"Call if you need me," CJ said. "Really."

I tried to say thanks but nothing came out.

# eleven

"Zoe!" Colette yelled. "Are you off? I really need to call —"

She stopped on the second to bottom step, her hands on her hips, because Daddy was in front of her. Elvis sat down on Daddy's work boot.

"Well," Daddy said.

Anne Marie and Bay stopped drilling vocabulary.

"Well," Colette answered.

"Is it gone?"

Colette said nothing. Devin snuck out of the den and sat next to me on the floor against the couch in the living room. "It's not," Devin whispered to me.

"I know," I whispered back. "Shh."

I could see Mom's feet come down to the landing. "Arnie," she said.

"I'm handling this." His voice was quiet and sharp. "Lift your shirt."

"Excuse me?" Colette asked.

Daddy spread his arms. "Did you think I would forget?"

"Come on, Arnie," Mom said. "We agreed."

"Lorna? Do *not* undermine me."

Colette's fingers pinched the bottom hem of her T-shirt. Stay still, I tried to ESP to her — Mom will get Daddy to leave you alone, if you shut up and let her handle this. But Colette narrowed her eyes and said, "I will *not* lift my shirt for you."

"Now!" Daddy yelled. "Do you hear me?"

I felt Devin grab my hand. I squeezed back and prayed for mental telepathy.

"I hear you fine," Colette told Daddy in her too-calm voice. "But you have no right —"

"I have no right? I have NO RIGHT?"

"That's what I said. I guess you can hear me, too."

"Don't you be fresh to me," Daddy growled. His huge bread-kneading hands were clenching and unclenching. It occurred to me he could punch her. *Please,* I prayed. *Please, don't.*

Colette's cheek muscles flexed but she didn't answer him back. We all waited and hoped.

"Apologize to your father, Colette," Mom suggested. "Now."

"No!" Colette spun to face Mom. "He has no right to —"

"To discipline my own child?" Daddy kicked the step.

Colette flinched, but then yelled, "I'm not a child!"

"Am I supposed to ignore it when my daughter comes into my house with her body mutilated?"

"I am not mutilated," she screamed. "I like how I look!"

"You look like a whore!" Daddy yelled.

Colette blinked twice and started to cry, which I could tell really infuriated her because she sucked in her bottom lip and bit it. She didn't wipe the tears away. She stood still and stared hard at Daddy, who was staring just as hard back at her.

"I hate you, too," she said softly.

Daddy covered his face with his hands. He breathed in, then out, very loud, and then stayed there, hidden in his own palms for a while. I wondered if he was praying.

When he finally dropped his hands, they were shaking. "Sweetheart . . ." he said, reaching for Colette, toward a big round tear that was tracking down her cheek.

She swatted his hand away with a fierce slap. Elvis growled.

"Colette," Mom warned. "Now, let's all . . ."

Colette didn't look away from Daddy's eyes. She spoke very slowly. "You have no right to touch me. Ever again."

She sniffed once, then cocked her head to the side and lifted the bottom of her shirt a tiny bit, so the little gold hoop showed. I couldn't believe it.

Colette turned quick and sprinted up the steps.

Daddy chased her, snarling, "I'll tear that thing out!"

As Colette made the turn around Mom at the landing, Daddy lunged for her, but he got tangled in Elvis and fell.

Devin and I were holding on tight to each other, praying for him not to have a heart attack and for Colette to get away.

Daddy pushed himself back onto his feet and charged again up toward Colette, but Mom stepped down to stand in his way and screamed, "Stop it! Enough!"

Colette's door slammed. Daddy punched the wall.

"What were you planning to do, Arnie?" Mom demanded. "Really! Rip it off her? And then what?"

Daddy mumbled, "Come on, Elvis." Together they slunk down the steps and disappeared into the kitchen. The back door slamming was like an echo of Colette's.

## twelve

I leaned against the door of Bay and Colette's room, my wet hair dripping over my shoulders, and waited for Colette to answer. Devin was in the shower, and everybody else was downstairs already, eating breakfast.

Colette turned around slowly and I saw she was sort of smiling. "Sure," she said. She pulled a brown T-shirt out of her drawer and held it toward me. "Brown is your color."

I hesitated for a minute. "I have Barbies that would be tight on," I protested.

Colette threw the shirt down on her bed. "Don't wear it, then." She whipped off her nightshirt and reached back into the drawer to pull out a blue-and-white shirt for herself. As she tugged it over her head, I had a chance to check out the hoop through her belly button. The skin around it still looked pretty angry.

I picked up the brown shirt. "I'll try it."

On my way out, I heard her say, "Zoe?"

"Yeah?"

"It's your body," she said. "You have nothing to apologize for."

"OK. You all right?" I couldn't look at her while I asked.

"Sure," Colette answered. "I blow off anything he says. So what if he hates me?"

"Well, if you need, or, I'm sure he doesn't really, don't worry," I stuttered, backing into mine and Devin's room. I heard Colette kick her dresser. I guess I wasn't too helpful.

While I hooked my bra and used Devin's deodorant, I thought about last night's dream. It was gym class, and gorgeous Mr. Brock put me on the boys' team despite all my protests until I pulled up my sweatshirt and screamed, "Look at these, would you? I'm a girl! I want to be on the girls' team!" Usually I don't remember my dreams but this one was pretty extreme.

I pulled on some white shorts, then sat down on my bed next to Colette's T-shirt to put on my socks and sneakers. I took a deep breath and thought, *If I ever want to try to be a different kind of girl, this is my chance to change. Enough of being one of the guys, buddies with everybody, never draw attention to myself because I'm just a jolly old team player. I have to do this.*

That made me smile. Please, it's just a shirt. Plus it's brown, with a little daisy on it in front. Sometimes lately I make such a big deal of nothing. Probably nobody would notice anything different from how I usually dress. It wasn't a glittery pink leotard or anything like I thought I was a beautiful star.

"Hey," said Devin when I reached past her to grab an English muffin off the dining room table. "Nice boobs."

I stopped. "Do they show too much?"

Anne Marie, Bay, and Devin studied my chest. "They sure show," said Bay.

"Why not?" decided Anne Marie. "Why should you wear stuff six sizes too big all your life?"

"Well," Devin said, "the boys will love it. Hey, Tommy!"

I looked away. Devin always seems to know my secret thoughts. CJ is lucky to have her own room so nobody can get inside her head.

We grabbed our lunches. "I hope I don't sweat," I said, checking my underarms. "There's no place to hide in here."

We were on our way out the back door, and Mom had already said, "Don't forget your lunch," when Colette joined us.

"Daddy didn't come home," Anne Marie said at the corner.

"Good," said Colette. They all piled onto their bus.

When my bus finally came, I sat down next to

Gabriela, my nice but boring cousin. Tommy and Jonas stormed on just as we were pulling out. They're lucky the bus driver is friends with their mother, or she wouldn't have waited for them. She's nasty. They slid into the seat ahead of me and Gabriela.

I tapped Jonas on the head. "You do the French?" Anne Marie had helped me with it in our frightened, quiet house after the fight, because Bay couldn't concentrate on vocabulary and Anne Marie would rather work than deal.

"You're talking to us again?" Jonas turned around and I guess noticed what I was wearing because he said, "Whoa."

Tommy turned around to see, too. I crossed my arms over my chest but his eyes had widened already. They faced front again. I sank down into my seat and whispered to Gabriela, "Do I look like a — I mean, gross or slutty or something?"

She shook her head. "You look pretty," she said.

"Thank you." She's so nice.

"If I had a bust," she said too loudly, "I'd show it, too."

I crossed my arms tighter.

None of my friends said anything as I climbed up onto the wall. I was tempted to curl into myself and hide, but what Colette said about not having to apologize kept echoing in my head and forcing my arms down. It was hard. I felt so noticeable.

After the second bell, I walked through the corridor toward our lockers, with CJ, Morgan, and Olivia. I could hear the boys behind us saying, "Do it, do it." I felt a touch on my back, and before I could turn around to ask, "What?" my bra strap snapped.

"Ow," I said.

"Ignore them," CJ whispered, linking her arm around mine.

"OK." I ducked my head and felt my face getting hot.

Another touch, another sting. "Ow!"

CJ yanked me forward before I could turn around.

"Puerile jerks," Olivia whispered.

I don't know what that means, so I shrugged noncommittally.

"If you say anything," Morgan whispered, "you'll just encourage them."

We were almost at the lockers. *If somebody pestered me over anything but my chest*, I thought, *I would knock him down and make him stop. Why is this different?*

As soon as I felt the next touch on my back, I spun

around and found myself eye to eye with Tommy Levit, whose hand was reaching toward me. His smirk was the same one I had found irresistible, yesterday. I almost punched him in it. But then I realized, this is exactly the problem with me; I'm so unladylike. The whole point, honestly, was to show Tommy I'm a girl. I tried to imagine what each of my sisters would do in this situation.

I stood as strong as I could and gave Tommy a nasty look.

Then I turned and walked toward the lockers, feeling proud of myself. My sisters, I think, would have given dirty looks like that. When Anne Marie glares, or Morgan, I die. Good for me.

Two steps later, I felt his hand on my back again.

I whirled around, pointed right in his face, and said, "If you touch me again, I'll rip off your thing and staple it to your head."

He stopped grinning. They all did. That whole pack of boys turned pale. It was great. I walked as confidently as I could to my locker and tried to open it, but my hands were shaking too much. I gripped the lock and closed my eyes.

"Yes," said Olivia. She bent over to use her key in her lock. When she stood up, her huge smile showed all her crowded teeth. "You tell 'em, Zoe."

"Yeah?" I asked her.

"Wow," CJ agreed. "Where'd you get that expression?"

I shrugged. "He looked surprised, huh?"

Morgan nodded. "It was pretty graphic."

"He won't be bugging you again," Olivia slammed her locker. "Score one for girl power."

She held up her delicate little hand. I high-fived it.

"How'd it go last night?" CJ asked. "With your dad?"

"Oh, that's right." Morgan looked at me with sympathy.

Not what I felt like discussing. "A comedy," I said, dismissing the subject with my hand like it was a bug. I wanted to get back to what a great job I'd done putting Tommy in his place. It wasn't what my sisters would've done, except maybe Colette, but obviously Tommy wasn't going to like me anyway, so, tough. "You don't think I was too harsh?"

"Well," Morgan said.

"What?"

"Nothing." She raised her eyebrows at CJ.

CJ jammed her lock closed and turned her back to Morgan. She leaned toward me and whispered, "Don't listen to people who lie."

Morgan backed away.

I nodded and stood up straight, like CJ, determined not to be one of those tall girls who folds herself into a parenthesis. I don't lie. Well, not too much. I try not to. I try to be a really good friend, unlike some people. I held up my head. Nothing to apologize for.

## thirteen

Morgan was kneeling on the bench, her lunch bag still unopened. "It was a little harsh, is all I'm saying."

"He deserved it," Olivia argued.

"But you know how boys are," said Morgan, blowing her bangs. "They were just kidding around. You have to have a sense of humor."

I took a bite of my sandwich and asked CJ, "What do you think?" I was psyched she was on my side, not Morgan's, this time.

CJ shrugged. "I guess he deserved it. You want me to put your hair in a bun? I think it would look pretty."

"OK." I tucked my limp hair behind my ear. It's really time for me to get a style, I guess. CJ stood up behind me. I crouched down a little so she could reach my head.

She tugged my hair away from my face and twisted. "Hand me two pens?" she asked.

I handed her both Bics out of my pocket and CJ stuck them through my hair. It hurt for a second but then it was OK. I took a bite of my sandwich while she looked over her work on my head.

"Pretty," she said.

I touched the bun. It was holding, maybe even elegantly. My neck felt naked. Across the cafeteria I could see the boys surrounding Tommy, staring at us. I tried to sit up straight.

"He deserved it but what?" I asked CJ.

"Nothing," CJ said, bending from her waist to pick up the napkin I had dropped. "The only thing is, you don't want the boys to think you're, you know, coarse."

"No," I agreed. I took the napkin from her and shoved it in my lunch bag.

"It looks pretty," CJ said. "Don't you think?"

I turned toward Morgan and Olivia. "Pretty," Olivia said.

"I think Tommy's upset," Morgan said, passing me her bag of Chee·tos. "You really humiliated him."

"Really?" I took a handful. "By saying to stop?"

"His 'thing'? And you were pointing at him, which is pretty rude." Morgan took a Chee·to, then offered some to Olivia.

"No thanks."

"CJ?"

"Can't. Ballet starts Saturday."

Morgan held the bag toward me again.

I shrugged and helped myself. "But don't you think he was asking for it?"

"I'm just saying."

"I know," I said, though I wasn't sure I knew anything. I mean, it's not like I revealed something personal, like, you're afraid of thunder! "It was just a crack," I explained. "It was just, like, *cut it out!* Tommy definitely knew that."

"Definitely?" Morgan asked. She looked over at the boys.

"We're buddies," I said. "We always rag on each other. I mean, I didn't take it personally that he was flicking my bra strap."

"No?"

"Well, not too personally."

"Listen. Can I be totally honest?" Morgan asked. She leaned toward me with her gentle brown eyes focused on mine.

"Uck," I answered. "If you have to be."

Morgan took a deep breath and said, "Look what you're wearing."

I crossed one arm protectively over my chest.

"That's not fair," CJ protested quietly.

"Sorry," Morgan said. "But she's one of my best friends, I owe it to her. All I'm saying is, don't you think maybe you were, a little bit, asking for it, too?"

"I don't know." I pushed my sandwich away. I couldn't eat any more. My crossed arms weren't having much success squishing my bust back into my body. "I didn't mean anything."

CJ touched my back gently. "Maybe you should tell him that."

"You think?" I felt too confused to have opinions of my own, right then. I just wanted to go home and hide in Big Blue.

"You don't want him to hate you, do you?"

"Definitely not." *In fact, I want the opposite.* "So I should what? Apologize?" I was sure she'd tell me not to be ridiculous.

CJ nodded. "Yeah."

"I agree with CJ," Morgan said.

Olivia shrugged. "I'm not really friends with them."

"If you'll come with me," I bargained. I wasn't sure at all what I would be apologizing for. I'm sorry everybody is mad at me, maybe.

"Of course," Morgan said. We all stood up and crumpled our lunch things. Morgan pitched my bag into the trash can. She has a very good arm.

"You sure?" I looked at CJ. Going over there to apologize was about the last thing in the world I wanted to do, but I wanted to make things OK again — with Tommy and also with them. Obviously I'm clueless on social problems, suddenly.

CJ smoothed my hair and whispered, "Mmm-hmm. Don't worry. We're right behind you."

## fourteen

The boys stood behind him and the girls stood behind me. It had taken about a month, it felt like, to cross the room to his table. I touched the side of my hair — still up. Too bad, because I could've used something to hide in, especially since I could feel dampness spreading cold under my arms. Please don't let me look like a total lunatic, I prayed, but, taking stock of what stood there in front of the boys, I felt pretty doubtful — sweat stains, tight shirt, pointy boobs, pens in my hair. How attractive.

"So, um . . ."

Tommy squinted up at me like he was surprised to see me standing there or like I was blurry.

"Sorry," I said.

He gave me one of his *don't be an idiot* faces. "For what?"

"For threatening to rip off your, you know, thing."

Some of the boys laughed. Tommy's fist splayed out to the side and caught Gideon in the belly. They stopped laughing.

We all just waited. I finally shrugged and started to turn away. If he doesn't forgive me, what can I do? I apologized. That would have to be good enough. I can't force him to like me. Obviously. Unfortunately.

Tommy's voice stopped me. "It was the part about stapling it to my head that got me."

I turned back around to see him grinning.

"Yeah, well . . ." I smiled, too.

He stuck out his hand and said, "Truce."

I shook his hand. It was a little clammy. "Truce," I agreed.

CJ, Morgan, Olivia, and I went outside and sat under the chestnut tree to go over what had happened. We tried to remember every word and figure out what he meant by it, and what the other boys were thinking, and if they all thought I was coarse or not.

"Probably they think she has a lot of class," CJ said. "Coming over and apologizing like that." She smiled at me.

Olivia picked up a chestnut and rubbed the smooth concave part with her thumb. "I think he should've apologized, too."

I shrugged, just relieved I did it and hoping no-body would be mad at me anymore. I didn't need an apology.

"He took it really well," Morgan said, ignoring Olivia.

"Yeah," CJ agreed. "He didn't make a big deal, you know? He handled it like it was nothing, almost."

{159}

"You like him, don't you?" Morgan asked.

CJ buried her head on her knees.

"Don't you?" Morgan repeated.

CJ lifted her head just enough to let her eyes peek out, then hid again, and, without looking at us, nodded.

"I knew it!" Morgan said. "You can't hide anything from me."

I pushed CJ on her shoulder. "I knew it, too!" I wore a big smile. That's great, if she likes him. She's cute; he probably likes her, too. How nice.

Meanwhile, CJ wouldn't pick up her face. We all pushed her until she toppled over and, giggling, said, "OK, OK! I admit it!"

We tightened our circle to talk strategy.

"I can't believe I like him, he's so sarcastic and obnoxious, but I do, I really like him," CJ whispered. "What should I do?"

Our foreheads were practically touching. "We have to plot," Morgan said.

"Right," I agreed.

"You really like him?" Olivia asked. "Because he definitely is obnoxious."

"Not all the time," I said. "But sometimes. Often. He is."

"What are you saying?" CJ asked me. "I shouldn't like him?"

"No," I said. "I'm just, weird." I pulled the plastic piece off the tip of my shoelace and chewed on it to keep from talking.

"What should I do?" CJ asked me.

I tried to think of what a best friend would say. "Um," I said. It felt like a big responsibility. I wanted to be a best friend to her. "You want me to do something?" I offered.

"No! No, no, no. Oh, promise me you won't tell him!" CJ's pale cheeks flushed and her green eyes bored right through mine. "Seriously. What if he said he doesn't like me? I'd die."

"OK," I agreed. Fine by me. "You can trust me."

CJ nodded seriously. "I know I can."

"We won't tell anybody," Morgan said calmly. "But maybe Zoe's right. She could sort of hint to him, and then he could, you know, think of it himself, and ask you out."

We looked at one another. Nobody came up with an objection to that plan. Except me, one little point. "Me?" I asked.

Olivia shrugged. "You got him to ask out Morgan last year."

"You're best friends with him," Morgan said.

"I am not!" I wanted to be clear. "He's not my best friend."

"Whatever," Morgan said. "You're better friends with the boys than anybody else, so . . ."

"Don't do it unless you want to," CJ said. "She doesn't have to."

"No." I smiled. "I want to. It's just, you know, if he thinks I'm coarse, you might not —"

"Oh, no," Morgan jumped in. "I don't think he thinks that. That's history. Everybody's over it. Right?"

"Right," CJ assured me.

"And maybe then," Morgan said, bringing her knees up to her chin like CJ, "maybe you could ask Jonas about me?"

"I knew it!" CJ said. "Excellent!"

I smiled and nodded. Excellent.

"But be subtle," Morgan added.

"I'll try."

For the rest of lunch we talked about how fun it would be if CJ and Morgan were going out with Tommy and Jonas.

## fifteen

When we got in to English, there was a paper lunch bag on each desk. I sat down and opened mine — nothing inside. I looked up at Mrs. Shepard to see what was going on. She has a reputation of making people cry, but I really like her. She's about four feet tall and built like she was put in a trash compactor. She takes no crap. Some people call her the Sadist but I feel like, hey, at least she believes we're capable of actual thoughts.

She stood in front of the class tapping the pointy toe of her shoe, touching her tongue to her upper lip. Devin said when she was in seventh grade, she never heard Mrs.

Shepard yell, all year. She could kill you with a lifted eye-brow.

We quieted down pretty quick. "Your homework over the weekend . . ."

A few people groaned. I knew better; my sisters had all warned me.

"Is there a problem?"

Lou Hochstetter raised his hand. She didn't call on him, just looked surprised in his direction. "Usually teachers give us the weekend off." When she didn't look any less surprised or more angry, Lou went on. "To recu-perate."

Mrs. Shepard raised one eyebrow at him. I think she melted him because he shrank in his seat. He sits right in front of me, and I swear, he contracted.

After about a minute, Mrs. Shepard said, "Well, Mr. Hochstetter, welcome to the seventh grade."

We all sank a little lower in our seats.

She waited another minute. The clock in her room ticks incredibly loud. "Your homework for this weekend," Mrs. Shepard said again, exactly as she had said it the first time, no added anger or stress. "Is called Bring Yourself in a Sack."

Nobody was budging so she went on. "I'd like you to gather ten items, over this weekend, which will all fit into the bag on your desk, and which, combined, will represent you in your many aspects."

I looked at the bag on my desk. Put myself in it? I tried to think of what could represent me. Big Blue? My sisters? My framed certificate from being sixth-grade class president? All too big. Hey, maybe Colette's brown

T-shirt. It was a small lunch bag, but the shirt was feeling pretty microscopic. I tugged to stretch it. No, this shirt is not me at all.

Mrs. Shepard, sensing that nobody was about to ask any questions, continued. "This is the beginning of our first unit on creative writing. We'll be exploring different ways of portraying characters. So, for today, I'd like you to split into pairs and interview each other. You'll then write a newspaper-style article on your partner. Get details like significant events in your subject's life, favorite foods, what nobody knows about the subject. . . . Be creative, ask probing questions."

She stopped talking and touched her tongue to her top lip again. We just sat there. "Is there a problem?" she finally asked.

I wasn't coming up with any complaints, that's for sure. I looked over at Morgan, who was asking CJ to be partners. "OK," CJ said, then turned and saw me watching. "Can you get Tommy?" she mouthed.

I doodled on my paper. People started pushing their desks toward other people. Tommy sits next to me, so I turned to him and said, "So?"

"Sure."

We pushed our desks head-to-head and opened our notebooks. "You want to go first?" I asked.

"OK." He poked his notebook with his erasable pen. "Hello. Name please?"

"Come on." As if he doesn't know my name.

He leaned forward and said quietly, "If the Sadist is half as rough as you, I'm not taking any more chances today."

I shrugged. "Fine. Zoe Grandon."

He wrote down my name. The Z looked like a big number three. "How much do you weigh?" he asked.

"Shut up." Probably more than him. I crossed my arms over my bulging chest.

"I'm just trying to get the inside scoop, ask probing questions."

"No comment."

Under where he'd put down my name, he wrote, "Sensitive about her weight." I can read upside down, although his writing is very pointy. I sank so low I was practically horizontal.

"How about we take turns asking," I suggested. I didn't think I could handle being on the spot without a break.

"Fine," he said, grinning. "Ask me anything."

I looked down at my paper and chewed on my pen, and without looking up asked, "Do you like anybody?"

"Almost everybody," he answered.

I gave him a half-smile, like, cute. "But do you *like* anybody."

"Oh," he said. "Um, well, sort of. Yeah."

I looked up at him. He looked down at his desk and sucked in his cheeks so his dimples showed. I wrote down, *Tommy Levit likes* _____. My writing is much rounder than his. I took a deep breath and asked, "Who?"

"My turn," he said.

"OK."

"Do you like anyone?"

"Yes," I admitted. My legs both started shaking. "My turn," I said, crossing my legs to keep them from slamming into anything. "Who is it?" I asked. "For you. That you like?"

"No comment," he answered, crossing his ankles. "Who do you like, like?"

*If you only knew,* I thought, but I whispered, "No comment, also." We were both talking really quietly.

He licked his bottom lip.

I asked, "Is it . . . someone I know?"

He nodded and looked up at me without grinning. He had never looked at me quite like that before. We were staring at each other.

I licked my lips, too, but my mouth was suddenly so dry it didn't help. I looked down at my notebook. *Mention CJ,* I told myself. *If you want to be a best friend, here's your chance.* "Is it —" I couldn't finish. I squeezed my eyes shut. *Don't ask him what you're really thinking. Don't ask him, Is it me? Because if you ask, Zoe, and he says, No way, you will never be friends with him again.*

He scuffed his sneakers against his chair and didn't prod me to finish asking my follow-up question. I prepared myself for him to ask me if he knew the person I like. I clamped my mouth shut so his name wouldn't pop out.

When I looked up, he was still staring at me. I flicked my eyes back down. Could he possibly be thinking of me? It felt like, suddenly, maybe.

I didn't want to move for fear I'd find out it was a fantasy. I wanted to enjoy the possibility for one minute. But before I could lift my eyes to his again, I interrupted myself with reality. *He'd never like you,* I warned myself. *Boys don't like you that way, remember? You're not pretty; you're just his friend. Go light. Give it up.*

He didn't ask me who I like. Probably wasn't interested, I realized. I doodled the word *if* on the corner of my paper, then scribbled over it.

I cleared my throat. "What's your favorite food?"

When he didn't answer, I let my eyes wander up to his again. He blinked, looked down, and shifted around in his seat. "I don't know. Pineapple upside-down cake."

I smiled at him. That's a normal Tommy answer, something weird and you can't tell if he's kidding. He wouldn't look at me, though; he stayed slumped in his chair. I doodled circles on my paper, tight circles in the blank of *Tommy Levit likes* _____, so the ink got deep dark blue. I doodled in *CJ* and then on top of it a Z for me, but nobody could see because I was doodling circles on top of circles over the letters and between them, and the letters *M-A-Y-B-E*, also.

When I realized I'd made a hole through the page, I tore it out, folded it up small, and pushed it to the corner of my desk. Garbage. There wasn't any usable information for my article on it. I doodled cartoon dogs on the next page until Mrs. Shepard said. "OK. Let's put the desks back. Please spend the rest of the period writing a newspaper feature about the person you interviewed, and leave it on my desk at the end of the period."

Dragging my desk back to its normal spot, I caught eye contact with CJ. I shrugged and looked away. I hadn't done a very good job — at being a best friend or an interviewer. I don't deserve her, I realized. Morgan would've fixed them up for sure. And not to let schoolwork intrude on my social life, but what was I supposed to write? I turned to a fresh piece of notebook paper and spent the next fifteen minutes writing down everything I knew from before about Tommy, like he's been working on his tennis serve and his mother embarrasses him and his twin brother is his best friend and he's proud of what a good older cousin he is. The introduction read: *Thomas David Levit says his favorite thing in the world is pineapple upside-down cake, but the truth is more complicated than that.*

When the bell rang I was still writing. A note dropped on my desk, but I pushed it aside and covered it with my left hand so I could finish. I stood up, still writing, and finished while CJ and Morgan waited at the door, saying, "Come on! Come on!"

I grabbed my stuff, slammed my two pages onto Mrs. Shepard's desk, and quickly unfolded the note. It said *For Zoe Only,* in Tommy's pointy writing on the front. When I saw what was inside, I refolded it and shoved it in my pocket.

"Anything?" CJ whispered, dragging me toward the lockers.

I shrugged. I couldn't talk.

"Did you hint? What did he say?"

"Nothing much." I pushed open the door of the girls' room. "Meet you in gym?"

"OK." She ran to catch up with Olivia and Morgan. I locked myself in a stall and unfolded the note again. It was my paper, the one I had torn out of my notebook, folded, and forgotten. Below the mess I had doodled, Tommy's erasable pen had drawn a new line and filled it in. Here's how it looked:

Tommy Levit likes ~~Zoe Grandon~~

Zoe Grandon

## sixteen

"**Z**oe?"

"Hey," I called to CJ, quickly refolding the note and shoving it back in my pocket.

"You OK?"

"Um, yeah." I unlocked the stall door and came out into the green glow of the girls' room. I couldn't get the grin off my face, so I pushed past CJ and dropped my books next to the sink to wash my hands. "What's up?" I asked, but I was thinking, *How am I going to tell her?* and, *How do I stop smiling like a lunatic?*

"You don't look so good," she said.

"No?" The bell rang. "We're late," I said, bending down to pick up my books. "We'd better run or we're screwed." Who said "screwed" recently? Oh, Tommy. I pictured him running up to the bus stop yesterday morning, saying he thought he was screwed. Tommy. He likes me! Me? Maybe we'd kiss at the bus stop.

"CJ," I started. I was so excited, it was practically bursting out of me. *I have to tell her,* I thought. *No! You'll ruin everything.* But somebody has to tell him yes, I like him, too, so he'll know it's OK to ask me out. Of course, that was the least of my worries. I was having some trouble thinking straight. I wished I could run to the high school and tell my sisters.

CJ reached out and touched my hands. "You look like you're going to cry," she said.

And then I did, I swear. I started crying. I slid down to the floor and cried, right in the middle of the best half-hour of my life. Bawled. So much for the problem of *how will I ever stop smiling.* CJ sat down next to me with her arm around my shoulder.

"I never," I blubbered. "Devin said everybody cries in seventh grade, but I was like, not me! And here, I didn't even make it through the first week."

"What are you talking about?"

"Never mind. The thing is, I know I'm not pretty."

"Oh, Zoe," she said. "Is that it?"

I shrugged. "I know you and Morgan think . . ."

"I do not!"

"That boys would never like me . . ." *But you are wrong! So ha, ha on you!* Obviously I didn't say that part.

"I never said that, Zoe," CJ said.

"Right."

"I didn't!" she insisted.

"Fine." I wiped my eyes.

"Is that why you wore that shirt today?"

I pulled my knees up to my chest and looked away from her. I didn't know I was angry at her until that second. I thought I was just avoiding saying, *Hey, Tommy likes me, and isn't that awkward, just as I was hooking him up with you?* But I could barely look at her, I was so mad. Why would I ever want to be best friends with someone who thinks I'm so undesirable?

She craned her head around, trying to make eye contact with me. "Because boys aren't going to like you just for, you know, your boobs sticking out. Not nice boys, anyway."

"No?" *Maybe that's not true,* I thought. *Maybe that is exactly why a very nice though occasionally obnoxious boy suddenly likes me. Although, if so, yuck.*

"No," CJ said. "They're going to like you, Zoe, I know they will. Maybe they'll have to get a little more whatever — mature, but they'll be lining up at your door, by eleventh grade, at the latest."

I shrugged. "Eleventh grade?"

She tapped my sneaker. "Because you are strong and funny and a great friend, and that's what truly matters."

"Maybe." Maybe that's what made Tommy like me — that I handled the bra flicking strong and funny, instead of wimpy and backing-down-girly. I do know how to be a friend, it's true — at least, usually. That's what I like about myself. And I guess that's what CJ likes about me, too, which, thank goodness. I mean, I don't like her for her looks. How boring would that be?

"I'm sorry," she said. "I would never want to hurt you."

"I'll bounce back," I answered. "Truce."

She smiled and we shook on it. Maybe what Tommy really liked was how powerful he felt when I crawled across the cafeteria begging forgiveness — after he was a jerk to me. The same thing just happened, sort of, with me and CJ. Here I am being horrible to her, stealing Tommy, and she apologizes to me. It made me like her more than ever. Weird. But it doesn't really work that way, I thought. If Colette had apologized to Dad last night, would he like her more? Would he have come home? Actually, yes, I bet he would've.

"It's not that, anyway," I whispered. "It's . . ."

"What?"

"Everybody thinks my family is so perfect, but the truth . . ."

She bent her head toward mine. "You can tell me, Zoe," she said. "I told you about my crazy mother and you kept it secret. Everybody's family is a mess. I swear, I won't tell a soul."

"Not like mine."

"What happened?"

I gathered my books into a pile. "We're gonna get detention for skipping gym."

"I don't care," she said. "You're more important to me than gym class. If something's wrong, well, then, I'm not budging."

I took a few deep breaths and let my math text slide off my loose-leaf. "Colette wouldn't show him her belly button. So he called her a whore," I said quietly.

She shook her head but didn't say anything.

"I mean, she asked for it," I explained. I didn't like the way I had just made my father sound and I don't want CJ to think badly of him. "He told her to get rid of it and he is her father. It's his house."

"It's her house, too."

"Yeah, but she knows what kind of reaction . . . My parents aren't exactly liberal."

"Still."

"She always does this." I shifted around so I could look at CJ and explain. It's so hard to explain, and I wasn't sure if I was just spilling all my family's secrets as an excuse for what was really going on with Tommy, or vice versa.

"What?"

"I mean, she could've just left it but she . . ." I lifted the brown T-shirt and showed my belly button, the way Colette had, last night. "She taunted him. She wrecks my family. I don't know where he went last night, but he didn't come home and I don't know if he's going to. He's never done that before."

"Wow."

"Yeah. I'm not allowed to tell this kind of thing."

"I won't say anything," CJ promised.

It felt so good to let it out I just kept going. "When my mom stands up for Colette, in the middle — she always does that, she thinks she's so fair, but, so my dad feels like, like a nothing, and I don't blame him. But I mean, Mom was just protecting Colette, which she should, she has to, it's her kid. And she was right, but . . . I don't know what's going to happen, but if they get divorced because of Colette, I swear. They give us everything. Do you know how much shoes cost, for five of us?"

"A lot?"

"And then Colette shoves it in their face. I hate her."

CJ nodded.

"And him," I said, then stopped. "No, I don't hate him. Or her, really, either. Hate. That's silly. I don't hate anybody."

"Of course you do," she said.

"No. I like everybody." I dropped my head into my hands and breathed my palms. The bun she had knotted into my hair came loose and when I looked to the side, a Bic pen was sticking forward near my eye. I yanked it out.

CJ laughed a little and smoothed my hair down my back.

"I was just so scared," I admitted.

"I bet."

"And when she said he has no right to touch her ever again?"

"Yeah?" She waited for me to explain.

"I mean . . . ever."

"She was mad."

"Still," I said. It was strange but that was the part bugging me most. It seemed so final.

"Well, you don't still hug your dad or anything, do you?"

"Sometimes," I admitted. "You don't?"

CJ shrugged. "It feels sort of, I don't know, creepy lately. But sometimes I do, I guess. If I'm tired. I didn't think you would."

"Maybe I'll stop hugging him in eighth grade," I said, wiping my nose on my hand.

CJ stood up. "Me, too." She ripped some toilet paper out of a dispenser and handed it to me.

"Toilet paper?" I asked.

She shrugged again. "I don't know what to do."

"You are such a good friend," I told her.

She sat back down next to me.

After a minute I told her, "I never heard my father say that word before."

CJ nodded. "Ouch."

"He must really hate belly button rings."

"Seriously," she agreed. "Wouldn't you die? If my dad ever called me a . . ."

"I know it. Me, too. Colette doesn't even care, though."

"Still," said CJ. "Not to knock your dad or anything, but it was pretty wrong of him, saying that. Don't you think?"

After I blew my nose I said, "Yeah. He was wrong." I took a deep breath. It felt better and worse at once, thinking it could be that simple, Dad could just plain be wrong. "But the thing is," I whispered, "I still love him."

"He's your dad."

"Right. Thanks." I blew my nose again and tossed the toilet paper into the garbage. "I mean it, CJ. I never tell anybody this kind of stuff. I'm really not supposed to."

"You can tell me anything," she said slowly.

I know," I said.

"I mean, like, I trust you." She pointed her toes hard. "Totally."

"So." I straightened my math text on top of my notebook. "You really like Tommy, huh?"

She nodded. "But don't worry. I'd never let a boy come between us."

"Neither would I," I promised.

"Do you think he might like me?"

"He should. He's stupid if he doesn't." I tucked my hair behind my ears. "Sorry about the bun."

"I like it better down, I think." She untucked it and the side fell forward. "It's more you."

"Whoever that is."

"That's my best friend," she said. "So you give her a break."

## seventeen

Most of the kids were already on the bus when I got out there. We hadn't been caught for cutting gym, at least yet, so CJ and I said goodbye at the wall, and I promised I'd call her later.

Jonas was three quarters of the way back, doodling in his notebook, and Tommy was across the aisle, also alone, looking out his window. I walked up slowly, hearing the doors creak shut behind me, and plopped down next to Tommy as the bus lurched forward.

Tommy didn't acknowledge my existence until after the first stop. "You cut gym," he said to the window.

I blurted out, "Do you like CJ?"

He turned and faced me like WHAT? I looked down, away, at my sneakers; I inspected the shoelace where it was fraying. She is my best friend. She is the best friend I've ever had.

Tommy picked at the callus he's been working on and asked quietly, "Did you read my note?"

"Hey, Zoe!" Jonas called from across the aisle. "We're going bowling tonight. You want to come?"

"I can't," I lied. I love bowling, and home was the last place I wanted to stay tonight. But.

"Oh," Jonas said and slumped back into his seat with his knees up.

"Because if you want to ask out CJ," I whispered toward Tommy's knees, "you should."

He didn't say anything.

It was the longest bus ride home. I pulled my poor

shoelace apart so bad, all I had left were spindly strings. That expression, *Thank God It's Friday*? Oh, yeah. At least I wouldn't have to face Tommy again for two full days.

I was standing before the bus stopped and had run halfway down the block before I heard the bus pull away. Tommy and Jonas always cut through my yard, though, so while I was fumbling with my key at the back door, they passed right next to me.

"See you tomorrow, maybe?" Jonas called. "You guys hitting tennis balls all day again?"

I looked at Tommy.

He was staring at me. "No," he said, and jumped the fence.

## eighteen

"You have to choose something about yourself to emphasize."

"I do?" I asked. I banged my feet against the under-sink cabinet and tried to choose.

"Yes," answered Colette. "Hurry. Daddy left a message that he's coming home at six and I want to be gone."

"Um . . ." I couldn't think what about myself to emphasize. My behind was getting wet from the counter. I had ripped off Colette's trouble-making brown Ace-bandage of a T-shirt and snuggled into Big Blue as soon as I got home. It felt like comfort.

Anne Marie came in and took a mascara out of the medicine cabinet. Colette asked her, "Do you think Zoe's eyes or her mouth? To emphasize?"

"Eyes," Anne Marie said. "Zoe has the best eyes in the family." She leaned toward the mirror to apply her mascara.

"How they *look*?" I turned to examine myself in the mirror. I never really noticed how my eyes looked before. I thought when they say all the time that I have the best eyes in the family, they meant my vision.

"Makeup?" Anne Marie asked me.

I shrugged. "Nothing better to do."

Colette was spreading eye shadow on my lids when the doorbell rang. Bay yelled, "Hey, Zoe! CJ's here!"

"CJ? Come up! We're in the bathroom."

As CJ climbed the stairs, Anne Marie asked me, "Do you like somebody?"

"Somebody likes her, that's what I think," Colette told her. "She won't admit it."

Anne Marie blinked her eyes and mumbled, "I gotta borrow that shirt sometime, Colette."

"It wasn't the shirt!" I yelled.

They both backed away a step. CJ pushed open the bathroom door slowly. "Zoe?"

"Come on in."

"Are you busy?" she asked.

"No." *Free as could be, that's me.*

"Because I could come back another time. I should've called."

"Don't worry about it. What's up?" Colette and Anne

Marie were still staring at me for yelling. I never yell. I prayed they wouldn't mention it in front of CJ.

"He asked me out," CJ said.

I guess I jumped because the eyeliner Colette had started stenciling me with made a jagged track down my face. "Zoe!" she complained, but I didn't care.

"What? When?"

"Just now," CJ said. She was trying so hard not to smile, she was frowning. "Before. He called me on the phone."

Devin pushed open the door and it slammed into CJ, who was catapulted toward the bathtub. Our bathroom is not huge; in fact, it's pretty cramped for just two people, but lots of times we all jam in. "Oof," CJ said.

"Sorry," said Devin, heading for the toilet. She pulled down her pants and started to pee. I noticed CJ blushed and looked away. We have no qualms in my house. You can't.

"That's OK," CJ mumbled toward the bathtub.

"Who asked you out?" Colette asked as she wiped eyeliner off my cheek.

"Tommy Levit."

"Tommy Levit?" Anne Marie asked. "I used to baby-sit them."

"He grew up," I said. I hate when she acts so adult. Please.

She pointed at my sweatshirt. "You ever wash that thing?"

"It's Big Blue," I explained.

Devin shook her head. "She never washes it. She's afraid it will disintegrate. It's her security blanket, practically."

"That's like you with Old Yellow," Anne Marie taunted Devin.

"Yeah, Devin," I said. She used to sleep in Old Yellow every night. It faded so much it wasn't even yellow anymore, just old.

Devin shrugged. "Maybe, but by seventh grade I was into boys, not sweatshirts, thank you very much."

"Give Zoe time," Anne Marie said. She took some blush and asked, "What are you doing tonight, Colette?"

"Staying out of Daddy's way."

"Good," Anne Marie said. Colette and Daddy hadn't crossed paths yet, and that was fine with everybody.

"Indeed," said Colette. "I was gonna hang out at Matthias's house."

"Matthias?" asked Devin, flushing the toilet. She pushed between Anne Marie and Colette to get to the sink. "You mean Matt O'Donnell?"

"He changed it," Colette said, weakly.

We all cracked up. "To Matthias?" I asked.

"Please," said Anne Marie. "Of all the pretentious . . ."

"You could call him Thigh Master for short," I suggested. I was happy to put Colette into the spotlight, rather than me and whether I liked boys or sweatshirts. Can't a person like both?

"Hey," Colette said. "You watch it, Zoe. Take a look."

I turned toward the mirror and blinked a few times. I looked older. It was hard to know for sure if I liked it. I do have nice eyes, I noticed.

"Has anybody seen my mascara?" Mom yelled from her room. Colette quickly closed the mascara and shoved it into the medicine cabinet.

"No!" we all yelled.

CJ smiled. "It's so fun, here."

Devin smudged on some concealer and left. On her way out, she warned Colette, "It's five-thirty."

"I know," Colette said. She quickly brushed some blush over my cheeks.

"You can just leave it at that," I told her.

"It's OK."

"It really doesn't matter how I look, anyway."

"You look good," CJ said. "Different but good." She perched on the edge of the bathtub.

"How did you get here?" I asked. "Is your mom downstairs?" I was picturing my dad coming home early with

Colette still up here and a great big Grandon family blowup performed especially for Mrs. Hurley. Not what I wanted at all.

"No," CJ said. "I was so excited, I just had to come tell you. I rode over on my bike."

"It's like five miles!"

She shrugged. "I had to tell you." She shivered a little in her flimsy T-shirt. You can see her collarbones, she's so thin. They made me mad. Skinny girls get the boys. Graceful, cute, sweet girls who are so good they'll ride five miles in cool weather to tell a friend exciting, terrible news. It made me hate her again.

*He liked me, not you,* I thought. "I'd last longer in the North Pole than you," I said.

"What?"

Of course, CJ had no idea why I was annoyed with her pretty, skinny little self. *Get over it, Zoe. He liked you. You made a choice. And she is a good friend. Your best friend. Be happy for her.*

"Like you're kissing," Colette instructed me.

"As if I knew how," I answered.

"Someday," Anne Marie said.

"So, CJ," I said, puckering, "Tell us what happened."

CJ smiled. "He called and asked me, over the phone."

"Verbatim," Anne Marie said to CJ.

"What?"

"Tell us every word," Anne Marie explained.

CJ looked thrilled. My lips were cramping.

"He said, 'Hi, CJ?' and I said, 'Yes,' and he's like, 'It's Tommy,' so I go, 'Hi,' and he's like, 'You want to go out with me?' and I'm like, 'OK,' and he goes, 'OK, see you Monday.' That's it!"

I looked down at my fraying shoelace and said, "That's great, CJ."

Anne Marie leaned against the counter. "Romance lives."

"What did you say to him, Zoe?" CJ asked. "You must have said something on the bus."

"I hinted," I said, and closed my eyes.

"You are such a good friend," CJ said.

Colette pushed my face from side to side, checking me. "You're gorgeous," she said. "And I'm out of here." She slammed her makeup kit closed, blotted her own lips, and said good-bye.

"Thanks!" I looked in the mirror at myself. I looked like I needed what Mom would call a good scrubbing.

Anne Marie said, "Well, I should study."

"She must be really smart," CJ said after Anne Marie left.

"She is," I whispered. "But she's not studying. She's looking out her window at the empty driveway, waiting to see if Chris Boyne comes by."

CJ nodded, knowingly. "We're all nuts, huh?"

"Yeah," I said.

"Except you, thank goodness."

"Right," I said. "Let's go to my room. You want to stay for supper? Because I'm not going bowling or anything, I'm just staying home, and Colette went out so, I mean, she usually sits next to me, if you want." I didn't add, and it's less likely Mom and Dad will fight if there's a guest.

"I can't," CJ said. She sat down on my bed and shivered. She looked so frail, hugging herself, that I took off

Big Blue and tossed it to her. "Thanks," she said, and put it on. "Is it true, what they were saying about this sweat-shirt?"

"No problem," I said. I took a red sweatshirt from my drawer. It's not silky like Big Blue, but it's still nice.

"It's so soft," she said appreciatively.

I nodded. Maybe I am growing up. It only bothered me a little to see her in it. I sat down on Devin's bed.

"Hey," she said. "Here's the other thing, and you can say no if you want. But I was thinking, I have ballet to-morrow but would you want to go on Sunday to Sun-dries and, if you want, get those friendship rings? With me?"

"Yeah," I said. "Yeah, sure."

She stroked Big Blue. "I'll never take mine off."

"Me, neither," I said. "Will Morgan be mad?"

She shrugged. I shrugged, too.

"Great." She stood up. "I should go — my mother doesn't even know I left and she'd kill me. I'm not supposed to ride my bike and take a chance of getting hurt, this time of the ballet season. I might really just quit. She drives me nuts. You didn't tell anybody, did you?"

"Of course not," I said. "You can trust me."

"I know it." She started taking off Big Blue.

"Wear it home," I offered. "It's getting cold."

"You sure?"

"Give it to me Sunday," I said. "Or you could keep it for a while, if you want."

"Thanks." She rolled up the sleeves. "Hey, did you say anything to Jonas about Morgan?"

*Give me back my sweatshirt,* I thought, but I smiled and said, "I didn't get a chance." I honestly don't think it would be such fun, her and Tommy and Morgan and Jonas, all going out. I imagined them walking in pairs down the corridor, past our lockers, and up the plank onto Noah's ark. I don't think Noah let any best friends join the couples for the ride.

"Well, whenever." CJ bounded across the room. "See you Sunday. It's so exciting, isn't it?"

"Yeah," I answered.

# nineteen

I stayed in bed the next morning until my stomach's growling became unbearable. The smell of Daddy's pancakes overwhelmed my plan to hide under my covers for the rest of my life. I pulled on the red sweatshirt and some socks and skidded down to the dining room.

"Well, the dead walk," Mom said. Her hair was already done and her makeup was all on. She looked pretty.

I sank into my seat next to Colette and then realized — hey! She's here, he's here. She's eating his pancakes. Nobody else seemed to be noticing, but then again there was food on the table and in my family, we are serious about eating. Dad placed three perfect pancake circles onto my plate, and Bay passed me the syrup.

"Did you have fun last night?" Anne Marie asked Mom. Mom and Dad had gone out to the movies, just the two of them. Usually they go with a group of friends, anytime they go out.

"Yes," Mom said, happily. "We even went out for ice cream, afterward. Like a date."

Across the table, Bay rolled her eyes. We all ducked lower over our plates. It's embarrassing when they act like teenagers.

"Who wants more?" Dad asked. "Anne Marie?"

"A small one," she said.

"Bay?"

"Sure."

"Devin?" He skipped her, I thought. He skipped Colette. What does it mean?

"OK," Devin said. He served her. I could feel Colette constricting in the seat on one side of me and Mom holding her breath on the other.

"Zoe?"

I held out my plate.

"Colette?"

"No thanks," Colette said.

Now nobody was breathing. A hunk of pancake weighed down my tongue.

"OK," said Dad. He lowered the pancake on his spatula to the plate. "OK."

"Maybe a small one," Colette said.

Dad smiled and found a quarter-sized one, which he placed on her plate.

Colette mumbled, "They're good."

He nodded. Mom looked like she'd won the lottery. She poured me so much juice it almost overflowed my cup. *Hooray, hooray,* I thought — *they're making it through breakfast. Please.* But at the same time, I guess I felt relieved, too. Mom says you have to celebrate the small victories. I gulped down my juice.

After breakfast I went back upstairs and snuggled into my unmade bed. When Devin came in, she screamed. So I screamed, too. She screamed again.

"What?" I was shaking.

"You gave me a heart attack!" she complained. "What are you doing here?"

"I live here," I reminded her.

"It's ten-thirty," she argued. "Are you sick?"

"No." I rolled over. There was no wallpaper for me to pick at, since we just have paint, so I spelled out *T-O-M-M-Y* in tiny letters on the wall with my middle finger.

"You're not going over to bug Tommy?"

"Nah." I stopped making letters, in case Devin could read it somehow.

"What are you doing today?" she asked.

"Not budging."

"All day?"

I shook my head. She sat down on the edge of my bed. I thought about telling her to go away but instead I made room for her.

"You like him, don't you?" she asked. "Tommy."

I nodded.

"Well?" Devin asked. "Does he like you, you think?"

I pulled his note out from under my pillow and handed it to her. I listened to the crinkling of the paper as she unfolded it. She screeched and hugged me from behind, then asked, "But what about CJ? Didn't she say last night that . . ."

"I fixed him up with her."

"After he gave you this?"

"She's my best friend."

"Congratulations," Devin said, standing up. "The hormones have kicked in."

I thought about that. "You think?" I rolled over to see Devin nodding. I sat up and gathered my blanket in my lap. "How long does it last?"

She shrugged. "Pretty intense, huh?"

"Please," I said. "I mean, one minute . . ."

"Right, and then the next, boom!"

"Exactly," I agreed. "I love him. Suddenly I'm this to- tal lunatic, thinking about him — I can't stop. Did you ever notice how cute his dimples are?"

"Uh-huh. But . . ."

"But," I echoed. "CJ's my best friend, and she said she liked him first. I mean, we're getting friendship rings tomorrow. CJ and I. So how could I turn around and . . ."

{215}

"Where?"

"The rings?"

"Yeah." Devin balanced one foot on top of the other and waited.

"Sundries."

"Oh, I saw those," Devin said. "You like them?"

"You don't?"

She shrugged.

"It'll just be good to have something of my own, for once."

"But won't CJ have the exact same ring?" Devin asked.

"Yeah, but . . . Never mind." Here I was thinking Devin of all people was understanding me so well. The one who tortures me most. I should learn already not to trust her.

"Trust me," Devin said. "You'll be sorry if you buy them. One person will lose her ring or stop wearing it or something. It happens every time. Honestly. You buy friendship rings, you're just asking for fights and trouble. Somebody ends up crying, and you know what, Zoe? It's gonna be you."

"What are you, a psychic?" I flopped down on my bed to face the wall and trace Tommy's name into the paint with my finger some more.

I heard Devin turn on her lighted mirror. Why do I tell her anything? I should just keep everything inside, not let anybody except CJ know the real me. I can tell CJ anything. She doesn't torture me with it, she doesn't lecture me and treat me like a baby. Her friendship is the most important part of my life. It's worth whatever it costs me.

The only thing I can't tell her about is Tommy. Who am I supposed to hit with? And tease? And beat at bowling? And, OK, I admit it — flirt with? I can tell CJ anything but that.

Devin switched off her electric mirror and left. I pulled my blankets over my head and stayed in bed. When Mom noticed me in there, I said I had a headache and needed to sleep.

"Oh, not you, too," she said.

"Why? Who else has a headache?"

Mom shook her head. "It's the beginning of seventh grade. I've seen this four times already."

I didn't move while Mom pulled my shades. "I can't even have a fake headache all to myself?" I asked her.

"Rest up," Mom said on her way out. "It's only September."

I stayed in bed all day, listening to the *thunk-thunk-thunk* of Tommy hitting a tennis ball against his garage door.

## twenty

**O**ur breath made little clouds on the display case in Sundries. Mrs. Dodge waddled over and asked, "Yes?"

In a confident voice, CJ said, "We'd like to see those rings, those two, please."

Mrs. Dodge touched the green and gold shiny one. CJ and I shook our heads. She touched the silver matte-finish one with the big fake diamond hanging off, and we shook our heads again. Finally she touched one of the silver rings with the knot in the middle, plain but beautiful no matter what Devin thinks.

CJ and I nodded, together.

Mrs. Dodge took her gnarled finger off the ring and closed the display door.

"We want them," CJ protested.

"Wait a while," Mrs. Dodge said. She reached under the counter and slid open what sounded like a cardboard door.

"We're ready today," I explained. "Really."

Mrs. Dodge shook her head and said, "I heard you. Relax." She pulled out a plastic Baggie full of silver knotted friendship rings. Spilling maybe a dozen of them out on the black velvet rectangle, she said, "Find your size, girls."

I spread them out and we looked. "So many," I said. Not that I thought the two in the display case were the only rings like that in the whole world, but a Baggie-ful under the display — Olivia could come in anytime and buy one if she wanted, too, and Roxanne, even Gabriela. Even Morgan.

"Doesn't matter," whispered CJ. I felt like she had read my mind. She picked up one ring and slipped it onto her finger. It was so big it slid right off when she tipped her hand. I picked it up and tried to wiggle it on, but it barely got over my first knuckle.

I dumped it onto the rectangle and said, "Oh, well."

"Oh, well," she said back. We laughed and kept looking.

We found one to fit each of us. The ring was lighter than I had expected it to be. *This is it,* I thought. *Something of my own. This is what I've been wanting.* I smiled at CJ, but then had to look away. I'd expected to feel completely happy, I guess, and I couldn't, not quite, not completely.

"This is what I'm putting in the paper bag," I said, touching the ring with my thumb. "Myself in a sack."

"Oh, I haven't put anything in yet, have you?"

"No," I lied. "Nothing yet."

"I'll put my ring in mine, too, OK?"

I shrugged. "Sure. I'd feel stupid if you don't."

"Great," CJ said. "This, and a toe shoe, and what else? You could put in, maybe, a tennis ball."

"I'm not that into tennis anymore," I said. "I don't just think about sports."

"I know." She twisted her ring around, admiring it. "Sorry. That's not what I meant."

"It's OK." I twisted my ring, too. This is what I wanted — to be chosen. Best friends. This friendship ring. Every time I get what I want lately, I burst into tears. To avoid that, I asked CJ, "How was ballet?"

She lifted her left leg and pulled it up with her hand, up over her head.

"Wow. Do you have any bones in there?"

She lowered her leg, smiling. "It was good, really good."

"That's great," I told her, "that you're feeling better about it."

"I don't know," she whispered. Mrs. Dodge shrugged and turned away. "I can't decide what to do and I'm not even sure if it's my choice. I have to talk to you about it later. She knows my mother."

"OK," I whispered back. I wanted to be helpful to her. She seems so far away sometimes, with her own life I know nothing about. My best friend, I almost bragged to Mrs. Dodge. We're best friends; we chose each other. "So. Did Tommy call you yesterday?"

"No," she said. "I couldn't stop thinking about him, all day. Well, except during dance class. But the whole way home, I was like, Tommy, Tommy, Tommy. You're lucky; you're so sane."

"Yeah," I said. "Good ol' sane Zoe." Sure. Like I spent the weekend thinking something other than Tommy, Tommy, Tommy.

"Seriously," CJ protested. "It's what everybody loves about you — you're so . . . balanced."

"Me?" I asked. I laid out my crumpled dollars for the down payment.

"You'll have to come in each week with two dollars, at least," Mrs. Dodge said, scooping up my money.

"No problem," answered CJ, paying hers.

"No problem," I agreed. "It's worth it." Did I need to convince Mrs. Dodge? Or who?

We each read the small type on an installment agreement. It felt so official and serious, like I should call a lawyer to look it over for me. Well, it is important; CJ had said so and I felt exactly the same. It's a commitment.

I watched my new ring bob as I signed my name next to the *X*. Before I passed the contract back across the counter, I underlined the rounded letters of my signature. *There it is. That's me,* I thought — just a little less pointy than the *Zoe Grandon* on Tommy's note, the one thing I'd put into my brown paper bag so far. But of course I'd never bring it in like that. Myself in a sack is obviously much more than a boy who put a worm on my head in kindergarten likes me. Liked me. Whatever. Please.

*I'll take the note out when I get home,* I thought, *and find ten funny, reasonable things to replace it.* A piece of French toast might be funny, a fraying shoelace, my jam-packed phone book with everybody in my whole grade's number and birthday filled in, this ring. Maybe I'll keep the note for a little while, though. I'll just hide it in the bottom of my sweatshirt drawer until I'm ready to throw it away.

## ABOUT THE AUTHOR

RACHEL VAIL has written four other well-received novels for adolescents including WONDER, an *American Bookseller* "Pick of the Lists," which Judy Blume called "Wonderful!"; DARING TO BE ABIGAIL, a *School Library Journal* Best Book of the Year; DO-OVER, a Recommended Book for Reluctant Young Readers; and EVER AFTER, which was one of the New York Public Library's 100 Best Children's Books in 1994.

She lives with her husband and young son in New York City.